Folk Tales From
The Serendib

Folk Tales From The Serendib

A Collection Of Sinhala Stories
Heard In Rural Sri Lanka

Retold by
Sunil Munasinghe

Illustrations
Vijay Mohan

TAMARIND TREE
Toronto

Tamarind Tree Books Inc.,
14 Ferncastle Crescent,
Brampton, Ontario. L7A 3P2, Canada.

Library and Archives Canada Cataloguing in Publication

Munasinghe, Sunil -, author
Folk tales from the Serendib : a collection of Sinhala stories heard in rural Sri Lanka / retold by Sunil Munasinghe; illustrations by Vijay Mohan.

ISBN 978-0-9919157-3-6 (pbk.)

1. Tales--Sri Lanka. I. Mohan, Vijay, illustrator II. Title.

GR306.M85 2015   398.2095493   C2014-905454-8

This book is manufactured under Sustainable Forestry Initiative® (SFI®) Certified Sourcing.

*To all storytellers who kept the tradition
alive for thousands of years.*

CONTENTS

Storyteller's Note   11

PART I
GAMARALA STORIES

1. Gamarala's Son Goes To School   16
2. Gamarala And The Buffalo   19
3. How Gamarala Went to Heaven   22
4. How Gamarala Watered His Garden   28
5. Gamarala's Half-Son And The Fly   30
6. Gamarala's Abandoned Daughter Becomes A Princess   33
7. Gamarala's Son-In-Law From The Netherworld   37
8. Gamarala's Donkey Minds The Dog's Business   41
9. Gamarala's Daughter And The King's Ring   43
10. Gamarala's Gift   46
11. Gamarala And The Pumpkin Thief   49
12. Gamarala And The Cow With Three Legs   51
13. Gamarala And The Foolish Leopard   54
14. Gamarala Finds A Son-In-Law With 'Thuththiri' Tree   56

PART II
ANDARE STORIES

1. How Andare Ate The King's Sugar   60
2. How Andare Lifted A Giant Rock   63
3. Andare Makes The Ministers Lay Eggs   65
4. Andare Makes His Wife And Queen Play Deaf   66
5. How Andare Ate The King's *Jambu* Fruits   68
6. Andare And The Tapper   70
7. Andare's Duel With A Giant   71

Contents

PART III
KING KEKILLE STORIES

1. King Kekille And The Audacious Thief 74
2. King Kekille's Deadly Morning Ritual 77

PART IV
MAHA DENA MUTHTHA STORIES

1. The Wise Man And The Head Of A Goat 80
2. Maha Dena Muththa In Search Of New Pupils 81
3. How Maha Dena Muththa Found The Missing Man 84
4. How Maha Dena Muththa Ended The Drought 86

PART V
RAKSHAYAS & YAKSHAYAS

1. The Ogre, Some Magic And The King's Illness 88
2. The Broken Drum 91
3. Jack Fruit - Gift From God 94

PART VI
ANIMALS & BIRDS

1. The Hermit Cat 96
2. A Foolish Donkey Dies In Bid To Become King 99
3. The Monkeys And The Hat-Seller 103
4. The Jackal And Its Crocodile Bride 105
5. The Flying Turtle 108
6. The Cobra, The Viper And The Mongoose 110
7. The Injured Horse 113
8. How The Hare And The Fox Ate Milk Rice 115
9. Magic Of The Magpie 117
10. The Trapped Deer And A Sly Jackal 119
11. A Foolish Bird And 'Mee' Flowers 123

Contents

12. The Lion And The Bull   125
13. The Farmer And The Cattle-Stealing Leopard   127
14. How The Jackal Got Rid Of Its Ticks   130
15. When The Fox Invited The Stork To Dinner   132
16. The Quails And The *Veddhas*   134

PART VII
OTHER RURAL STORIES

1. A Mother's Milk Is Never Measured   136
2. How We Got Sweet Potatoes   138
3. Seven Mendicants And A Pot Of Rice Porridge   140
4. The Flying Cotton Ball And A Greedy Cousin   142
5. The Golden Pumpkin   146
6. The Salt Seller And The Crafty Donkey   148
7. How Man Ended His Friendship With Elephants   150

GLOSSARY   152

STORYTELLER'S NOTE

Sri Lanka, an island covering an area of 65,610 square km off the southern coast of India, has a documented history spanning over 3000 years with a unique cultural heritage, rivaling any other ancient civilization in the world.

Though, on the surface, the island's culture looks like a spin-off of Indian traditions to a Westerner's eye, a closer look reveals distinct differences.

The two most important events in the island's heritage were the establishment of a kingdom by King Vijaya in 543 BCE and the arrival of Buddhism from India in 250 BCE.

The country's strategic location on a busy shipping route attracted traders and invaders alike, complicating the history of the island.

Greeks called the tear-shaped isle Taprobane and the Arabic traders who came for its spices named it Serendib while the Portuguese who landed in 1505 called it Ceilao, which became Ceylon to the British when they ruled the country from 1815 to 1948.

The term 'serendipity' which means an aptitude for making desirable discoveries by accident is based on Sri

Lanka's ancient name of Serendib.

Adventurers who passed through the island and invaders left lasting impressions on its heritage enriching the native language and folklore. Some folk tales bear a testimony to that foreign influence, with stories overlapping different cultures. Though the invaders were driven out, remnants of their cultures linger in the island's heritage.

Sri Lankans do not reject or revolt against such alien influences if they feel that they are beneficial, and have adopted them to suit their unique cultural identity.

It is difficult to relate folk tales to particular time periods but they certainly are based on value systems based on castes, beliefs, ethnicity, geography and many other factors, giving them a semblance of reality.

One unmistakable feature in folk tales is the old world charm where everything is uncomplicated. The stories are not too long and they are about simple people and animals confronting simple problems, with the solution lying within the story itself.

A story like 'Gamarala's Abandoned Daughter Becomes A Princess' embodies the magical qualities of a fairy tale with innocence triumphing over evil.

'Revenge Of The Magpie' evokes a movie effect like flashbacks, a rarity in folk tales.

The folktales in this collection are the stories I heard as a child from my mother, relatives and friends.

People passed down stories orally from generation to generation, often resulting in more than one version of the same story or with embellishments added by storytellers to attract the attention of their audiences.

Folk stories are probably not true but their relevance to the culture and time periods give the tales a quasi-historical value.

Many folk stories feature talking animals. This aspect

fits perfectly into Sri Lankan folklore because there was a belief that animals could talk at one time.

My great grandmother believed that animals could talk up to the time when King Vessantara, an earlier incarnation of the Buddha, gave away his two children to an old Brahmin to work as servants for his young bride. The King's wife, Queen Manthri, returned home from the orchard to find the children missing. She went to the jungle and asked the animals about the whereabouts of her children. The animals refused to talk although they had seen the man leading the children away. The belief is that from that day onward the animals lost their ability to speak as a result of the queen's curse.

The tale about how some men counted themselves after cutting wood in the jungle has many foreign versions but in Sinhala folk tales it is attributed to Maha Dena Muththa (The Elder Who Knows Everything) and his five disciples.

Maha Dena Muththa is a popular character in Sri Lankan folk tales. He is the opposite of Mahaushada Pandita, a sage in India who was known for his good counsel and sound judgment. Mahaushada also is described as an earlier incarnation of the Buddha.

Some versions of the stories in the *Panchatantra* which is a collection of Indian animal fables, originally written in Sanskrit around the 3rd century BCE, are featured in Sri Lankan folklore. *Panchatantra* tales and their cultural and religious similarities fit perfectly into the Sri Lankan milieu.

Many Sri Lankan folk stories are hilarious rather than being morality tales, complementing the islanders' penchant for a searing sense of humour.

These include stories about the Gamarala, the village elder, who is respected by the inhabitants. He is often portrayed as a wise man who becomes a tragi-comic figure because of the Gama Mahage's (his wife) foolishness.

The Andare stories are said to have emerged from the deep south of the island. According to a recent Sinhala book, Andare's real name was Andreas Silva, a famous poet with an infamous passion for impromptu verse (*Hituwana Kavi*). This legendary jester served in the royal courts of the ancient kingdom of Kandy, entertaining the kings.

In these pages, you will also read about King Kekille, also foolish like the Maha Dena Muththa. However, being the ruler, he had the power to execute people after passing ridiculous judgments.

There are no historical records to prove that a king by that name existed and mystery surrounds the origin of the name. Kekille is a common plant in Sri Lanka. It can also mean a name of a place or an imaginary country.

The stories in this collection have been edited for clarity and conciseness for foreign readers who may not be familiar with Sri Lankan folklore. However, care has been taken to preserve the originality and the context of each tale.

SUNIL MUNASINGHE
Toronto, November 2016.

PART I

Gamarala Stories

The Gamarala* is a popular character in Sri Lankan folk tales. He is someone who holds the *de facto* position of a village elder by virtue of his riches, comprising a swath of fertile paddy fields that required seasonal labour for cultivation and harvest.

The village economy grew around the Gamarala's rice paddies and most villagers who did not own cultivable lands were on his payroll. This position earned him prestige and an unofficial advisory role in village affairs. The people accepted his decisions without dissent, despite the dubious methods their beloved employer used to solve their problems.

As a result, the Gamarala occupied a unique position in many Sri Lankan folk stories, conjuring up images of a simple pastoral existence, dominated by the water buffalo and the plough. This individual had no family name and was simply known as the Gamarala, while his wife was addressed as the Gama Mahage, wife of the Gamarala. Illustrations in books of old show him dressed in a white vest with sleeves falling below his elbows, a striped sarong and hair tied in a knot at the back of his head.

Story I

Gamarala's Son Goes To School

The Gamarala's son was a strapping young man and had reached marriageble age when he got this sudden urge to go to school. The Gamarala and his wife were a little puzzled but agreed to go along with their son's decision.

The school was far away from the village. One morning his mother, Gama Mahage, cooked rice and wrapped it in a banana leaf as he set off early one morning.

"I have never gone to school. How do I study?" asked the son.

"It's very simple son. Repeat everything the teacher says. That's how your father studied," said the woman.

So the young man took the packet of lunch and left the house.

When he reached the school it was almost midday and the teacher was holding a class under a tree, teaching his pupils to write on sand with their fingers. All the students looked much younger than the Gamarala's son.

As he approached the class, the teacher asked him, "Who are you?"

Gamarala's son repeated: "Who are you?"

"What are you doing?"

"What are you doing?"

"Are you mad?"

"Are you mad?"

The pupils and the teacher burst into laughter. The Gamarala's son thought studying was very easy and sat under the tree for more lessons.

A pupil told the class that the new student was the Gamarala's son and the teacher became respectful to the boy though he acted funny. The Gamarala commanded much respect in the surrounding villages for his good deeds and the teacher was surprised to find that he had a half-witted son.

If he was just another student, the teacher would have caned him to make him obey orders and learn properly in the class.

In the evening, after school was over, the teacher told him to attend classes the next day too.

On his way home, the Gamarala's son felt hungry. He sat near a pond and finished his lunch. He felt sleepy after the meal and decided to climb a tree to rest for a while.

On the tree he began to mutter. He did not want to forget what he studied in school and repeated the teacher's words.

"Who are you?"

"What are you doing?"

"Are you mad?"

Soon he fell into a deep sleep. He woke up late in the night after hearing some voices below. Wiping his eyes with the back of his hands he looked down. His eyes were almost blinded by a blaze of light from the foot of the tree.

He looked through the leaves and saw three robbers trying to share a box of gold they had stolen from a temple. One robber was holding a lamp.

Gamarala's son did not want to forget the lesson and started remembering what he learnt on his first day.

"Who are you?"

The robbers were alarmed and looked up the tree but couldn't see anything. "What are you doing?"

They thought it was a wandering god who had made the tree his abode for the night.

"Are you mad?"

It was indeed a God trying to punish them, thought the robbers. They screamed in fright and took to their heels, leaving the stolen box behind. Gamarala's son climbed down, still repeating his lesson. He looked around but there was nobody. He hoisted the box of gold onto his shoulders and walked home.

His parents were about to send some villagers out to look for him as the jungle road was not a safe place to walk in the dark. They thought he had lost his way and wandered into the jungle where there were elephants and leopards.

The son eased his box of gold to the ground, leaving his parents and the search party speechless. "What happened, son?"

"All of this is the result of what I studied in school today," he said.

"Son, some people have to study a lifetime to acquire such wealth but you have achieved it in one day. Such is the power of education," said the Gamarala. "There is no need to go to school anymore."

Story II

Gamarala And The Buffalo

The Gamarala and a farmer were walking one day through a jungle and saw a buffalo. They lassoed the animal, tied it to a tree and petted it for some time so that it would get used to them. The farmer questioned the Gamarala about the ownership of the buffalo.

"We both saw it together and bunched creepers into a lasso and we both chased it and caught it. So it should belong to both of us," the Gamarala said.

The cunning farmer was unhappy with the decision but nodded his head: "Since I don't have a buffalo, I will claim the back half and you can own the front side."

The Gamarala agreed.

Next day, the farmer took the buffalo to his field and ploughed the rice paddies till evening.

Night passed into day and in the morning, the Gamarala went to the farmer's house to ask for the buffalo to plough his fields. The farmer allowed him to take the animal on the condition that only the forelegs should be used to plough because the hind legs belonged to him, according to their original agreement.

The Gamarala was furious. "In which world can a buffalo plough a field with only its front legs?" he shouted and left the farmer's house in a huff.

After some days, other inhabitants of the village complained to the farmer that the buffalo had wandered into their fields in the night and eaten their crops.

The farmer said: "Go and tell the Gamarala to pay you compensation because the front part of the buffalo belongs to him. Isn't the mouth in that part of its body?"

All the farmers in the village went to the Gamarala's house and quarrelled with him.

"Your buffalo is destroying our crops. I went to your friend and complained but he says that you are responsible as the front part of the buffalo belongs to you."

The Gamarala became very angry and went to the king and complained about the incident. The king summoned the Gamarala, the farmer and the affected villagers.

The king heard the story of how the two men found the buffalo and their agreement to share the animal.

The king wanted to deliver a fair judgement and he decided to cut the buffalo in half and divide it between the two men.

First he asked the Gamarala, who was holding a respectable position in the village, to come forward and kill the buffalo with a machete.

The Gamarala took the weapon, checked its sharpness with his fingers and paused. He looked at the king with tears in his eyes and said he did not have the heart to kill the animal. The Gamarala feared the wrath of the king for defying a royal order, but the ruler was calm.

The farmer was now thinking of the juicy chunks of buffalo meat that his family would soon enjoy. The man took the machete, raised it over its head and was about to deliver the deadly blow.

The Gamarala ran and grabbed the farmer's hand, "Don't kill this innocent animal. Take it away and be its owner."

The king declared the Gamarala as the rightful owner of the buffalo. The king ordered him to take the animal home and asked his ministers to gift more land to the Gamarala for the compassion he had shown to the buffalo.

He also ordered that the farmer be given a hundred strokes with the cane.

Story III

How The Gamarala Went To Heaven

The Gamarala loved his paddy fields. He loved to look at them during the rice planting season and during the monsoon and during the harvesting.

The first thing the Gamarala did after his early morning cup of tea was to go to the fields and look at them with affection, almost like a doting grandparent.

It was on one of these early morning rounds that the Gamarala was stunned to find some ripening paddy plants crushed and broken. It looked like a wanton attack and he stepped into the fields to examine the plants. The paddy stalks looked miserable, some broken in the middle, some twisted out of shape or smashed into the ground. Tears welled up in his eyes.

A sense of foreboding washed over him as he saw some strange markings resembling the imprint of a mortar (*wangediya**). The mortar was a wooden utensil that farmers used to crush paddy by beating it with a heavy pestle (*mol gaha**, or the milling tree).

Gamarala was convinced that the plants were destroyed by the mortar. "It is trying to exact revenge on me because of the beating it got from the heavy wooden pestles during the last harvesting season," he said aloud.

He rushed home, collected a pile of thick coir ropes and tied his mortar to the heavy wooden poles that held up the tiled roof of his house. "Aha*, now let me see how this mortar will go wandering into the fields tonight," he said.

The Gamarala could not sleep well that night. He tossed and turned and got up several times to look out of the window. The mortar was secure and tied up.

Early next morning, he ran out of the house to examine the area around the mortar. The heavy ropes were all in place, the knots as tight as ever. There were no muddy patches on the bottom of the mortar and no markings of any kind on the ground. It had not moved and the Gamarala let out a long, happy sigh.

After a leisurely breakfast of a rice dish and tea, the Gamarala sauntered out to his fields. His heart almost stopped beating. From a distance he could see that a large swathe of his paddy crop had been destroyed once again. Running into his fields, he saw the same markings on the ground that he had seen the previous day.

Anger rose like bile within him. His fists were clenched and he shivered. "I know, I know who did this," he shouted. The early morning breeze was gentle and the sunlight was just beginning to warm the earth. The Gamarala continued shivering.

With measured steps he marched home. He went into his barn and took down his big drum which was used only to warn villagers of some impending disaster. He began beating the drum furiously.

The villagers rushed to Gamarala's compound; men still groggy with previous night's jugs of palm wine and sleepy children still hanging to women's breasts.

It did not take much time for the villagers to understand the depth of Gamarala's anger but could not fathom what caused this violent reaction.

He told the farmers of the massive damage done to his fields by the mortars. He pointed to his own mortar still tied to the pole saying, "I cannot allow these mortars to take revenge on me for the beating they get from our women every harvest season. I tied my mortar last night so it had no freedom to roam but when I went to the field this morning more paddy plants had been destroyed. So rush home now and tie up all your mortars and make sure that they don't go anywhere in the night."

So the villagers went home and tied their wooden mortars with ropes to trees and some even dug holes and buried them and placed heavy rocks on top so that there would be no chance of them embarking on nocturnal wanderings as the Gamarala had suspected.

The next morning, the Gamarala went to the fields. More plants had been destroyed and more footprints could be seen all over the mud.

Gamarala went to every house in the village to inspect how best his vassals had secured the mortars. He checked every mortar to see whether there were any muddy patches. Satisfied that it was not the work of an errant mortar, the Gamarala decided to take matters into his own hands.

So that night, he went into the fields alone and hid behind a row of bushes vowing to remain without sleep until he found the culprit. The full moon shone in a cloudless sky and the silvery light allowed him to see far into the distance.

It was around midnight that the Gamarala heard a sound in the sky like some flying object hissing past and behold, it was a white elephant descending from the heavens glistening like a cotton ball in the moonlight. It landed quietly and began eating the maturing paddy plants, sloshing in the mud. Despite the raging anger that overtook the Gamarala during the last two nights, a feeling of veneration and calmness crept into his mind. A shimmering, silver elephant from heaven! Such events were the stuff of fairy tales. The Gamarala waited until the elephant ascended and disappeared into the clouds.

Still awake, the Gama Mahage sat on the doorstep, waiting for her husband. When he reached home she noticed that he was in a state of excitement. The Gamarala revealed to her every thing he witnessed last night.

"This is a golden opportunity to go to heaven alive. Many go their after their deaths but we don't have to wait that long," the Gamarala said. "We can hang on to the elephant's tail and hitch a ride to heaven."

The Gama Mahage who readily agreed to the journey was cautioned by her husband not to reveal the secret and their plan to anybody in the village.

The Gama Mahage, the good village woman that she was, could not hide a secret for a long time. Her mouth itched and scratched with the desire to tell the secret to someone. Her close friend was the washer woman who enjoyed gossiping about other people all day long.

That day happened to be the day of her biweekly visit to the Gamarala's house with another load of washed clothes and some juicy gossip about neighbours, collected from around the village well.

The washer woman noticed the air of excitement in the Gama Mahage household and surmised that the new cloth and blouse she was wearing indicated that she was ready to go on a long journey. The washer woman lingered around for a long time looking for some way to get the truth out of the Gama Mahage. The Gama Mahage capitulated at last and murmured into the washer woman's eager ears the happenings of the last few days and their planned trip to heaven.

The washer woman pleaded with the Gamarala's wife to take her and her husband along. "Look at my hands, my lady," the woman spread her palms to display the blisters and calluses caused by life-long washing of other people's dirty clothes.

When the Gamarala returned from the fields, his wife told him about the discussion she had with the washer woman. The Gamarala became very angry but kept quiet as he did not want to let things get out of hand. He forgave his wife with a sigh.

That night, the washer woman and her husband came to the Gamarala's house with a box full of food and snacks to eat on the way as they did not know how long the journey would last.

The Gamarala said there was no need for any food and all they needed for the trip were clothes they were wearing because heaven had everything they wanted. So the four of them went to the field and hid behind the bushes waiting for the elephant to descend from the sky.

Around midnight the elephant, in all its shimmering glory, landed on the field and began to eat the paddy stalks. The four of them were dumb struck by its size and beauty and as the celestial beast was getting ready to fly away, the Gamarala ran and hung on to its tail. The Gama Mahage held on to the Gamarala, the washer woman clutched her hands tightly around the Gama Mahage, followed by her husband.

Half way into the sky the washer woman looked down at the village disappearing under their feet and asked the Gamarala how big was the 'kuruniya'* (a container made of bamboo strips to measure rice) in the heaven. Not to be deterred by a foolish question from a foolish woman, the Gamarala thought he would describe heaven as if he had been there earlier and knew all about its many wonders.

"A *kuruniya* in heaven is this big," said the Gamarala stretching his hands wide to show the size of the vessel.

With that, all four of them fell back, thudding painfully into the slushy mud of the Gamarala's paddy field.

Story IV

How The Gamarala Watered His Garden

The Gamarala had a small parcel of land on which he grew a variety of vegetables every year. This garden, which was a family favourite, was irrigated with water drawn from a deep well. The farm, in turn, yielded plentiful crops every season.

One year, however, a severe drought caused all the wells in the village to dry up. Only the Gamarala's well had still a lot of water, because it was the deepest in the village. Of course, because of the depth, it was getting increasingly difficult to draw the water in a pail.

Every evening. the Gamarala and the Gama Mahage, irrigated the plants but after a few days, the Gamarala complained of exhaustion and muscle pain and gave up the effort. However, his wife continued to water the garden with great difficulty. She did not want the plants to die as they had already started to flower and sprout vegetables.

One evening, while tending to some plants, she saw two thieves crouching in the shadows behind some bushes in the corner of the garden. She silently left the place and told her husband about the two thieves.

The Gamarala went into the garden and called out aloud to his wife, "It's not safe to keep our gold and jewellery in the house. I have heard there are some thieves roaming in the area, looking for money and food. It's all because of this cursed drought. I know they will try to rob our gold soon. So, let us put all our valuable possessions in the well. It is very deep and no robber can touch them."

The two thieves heard what the Gamarala said. Early that night, they watched with glee as the couple dumped a heavy bag into the well. The two men could even hear the loud splash from the deep well as the bag hit the water, after what seemed a long time.

Such a heavy bag should have a lot of gold, thought the thieves. At night they crept into the garden and began to draw water from the well.

They emptied bucket after bucket into the earth and the water flowed joyfully through the vegetable plot, through the maze of channels and diversions, crafted intricately by the Gamarala. Dawn was breaking when they stopped work, vowing to come back the next night.

At night, they brought two more members of their gang to help them, but by dawn the well still seemed half full. This nightly labour of greed went on for a gruelling ten days, before the thieves got hold of the bag.

The four men hauled away the heavy bag into the jungle, loosened the knot and emptied its contents. The bag contained neatly arranged piles of round, black stones.

The vegetable plants thrived with the plentiful water and the Gama Rala had a splendid harvest and sufficient fresh produce to survive through the severe drought.

Story V

Gamarala's 'Half Son' And The Fly

One day, when the Gamarala was out in the rice paddies making arrangements for the harvest season, his wife, the Gama Mahage, asked her son to look for lice in her hair.

The son agreed as he had nothing else to do other than chasing butterflies and plucking wild berries from the shrubs surrounding the house. He was in his 20s but behaved like a 10-year-old and people said he was *tikak pissu*, a little mad.

Looking at him, the Gama Mahage would sometimes let out a long sigh and think aloud, "Oh, I must have done something wrong in my previous life to get a son like this. May be I have killed a son in a previous birth and he has come back to take revenge on me. Or he may be an ancestor who is reborn to trouble us for something we did without much thought. He can be even the result of black magic performed by villagers who envy our wealth."

She loved her son, and was thankful to him because he taught her to be good to other human beings. She could feel the pain of other mothers who had children with disabilities. He was born from her flesh and blood, and she despised her husband when he called him 'my half son.'

"We have to embrace with both our hands what *karma* gives us and learn to do good deeds to gather merits for the other life," Gama Mahage thought aloud. The son, in turn, loved her deeply, accompanying her wherever she went. He even threw stones at monkeys when they mocked her from the treetops.

She always asked her husband to go slow on his aggressive methods while acquiring land from the poor at throwaway prices. People pretended to be respectful in front of him, but they cursed him in private. She was kind to the villagers and became the calming influence, believing that this would mitigate some of the ill luck her husband's actions brought to the family.

She gave rice generously to needy villagers, inquired after their health and gave money when they wanted to buy salt, sugar and clothes from the Chinese trader who visited the village once a month to hawk things in his cane box. She bought clothes for children who had little to wear and visited the temple every Full Moon Day to observe *sil* - the Buddhist ritual of fasting till sundown - while praying and taking part in discussions of the scriptures.

She hated her husband when he drank palm wine and verbally and physically abused their son. It was the women who always suffered and paid for such *karmic* crimes, she thought. Their son was now of marriageable age but she worried that no woman would want to live with a manchild. She worried about what would happen to him when she died. Nobody lived forever.

The Gamarala suggested that he would find a woman to marry him in return for money and land as dowry. Gama Mahage, however, did not like the idea. It was always the

the bride's family that gave a dowry during a wedding and any change in the practice would make her family a laughing stock in the village. She sighed and wiped her tears. She would never be able to hold a granddaughter in her arms - she liked girls - hug her and smell the milky breath.

She rested her head on his son's lap and closed her eyes. He probed the roots of her hair with his fingers, pulling off lice and crushing each between the nails of his thumbs.

The Gama Mahage fell into a deep sleep. The son noticed a fly circling above them and settling down on his mother's face. He shooed away the fly with wide sweeps of his hands but the insect kept buzzing round his mother's face.

At last, he spoke to the fly, "Hey fly, please don't land on my mother's face. There are several dirty women in the village. Go after them." The fly circled with a loud hum as if mocking the young man and tried to land on his head, but flew in a wide arc at the last moment, landing this time on his mother's nose. Angered, the son lowered his mother's head slowly to the ground. He took a coconut coir broom and tried to swat it, but it twisted away and returned.

Gamarala's son ran out of patience. He took the pestle which his mother used to pound rice and brought it down with all his strength.

The Gama Mahage died instantly.

The fly was now setting itself down on one of the dry paddy stalks that made up the roof.

The infuriated son picked up several dry coconut leaves, bunched them together, set them alight and threw it at the fly. Within minutes the house was ablaze. The young man screamed for help and villagers rushed with buckets full of water to douse the fire but it was too late. A man ran to the fields to inform the Gamarala about the double tragedy. His son could guess what kind of fate awaited him at the hands of his father and he ran away into the jungle.

Story VI

Gamarala's Abandoned Daughter Becomes A Princess

The Gamarala's pregnant wife, the Gama Mahage, developed a craving for '*kekiri*'* melons, and weaved a reed bag to collect the gourds when they ripened on the vine.

The Gamarala went out every day, ate sweet '*kekiris*' to his heart's content without telling his wife that the melons were ready for eating. Judging by some seeds stuck to his beard the wife knew that the melons had ripened and her husband was eating them secretly.

One day, the Gamarala and his wife went to their fields that was in a clearing in a jungle and ate melons. On their way back, the Gama Mahage developed labour pains and gave birth to a baby girl. The couple did not want a girl child, so they abandoned the newborn near a pond.

Two cranes saw the baby girl and carried her into a cave. The cranes also had a parrot, a dog and a cat that soon became friendly with the little girl. They named her Biso (Queen) because the girl was growing up to be a pretty young woman. When Biso reached puberty, the cranes wanted to celebrate the occasion by presenting her with a necklace. One morning, the cranes left the cave in search of gemstones to make the necklace.

Before flying away, they advised Biso not to leave the cave as there was a she-devil called *Rakshi* living in the jungle. They also asked the girl to cook lunch and feed the pets as a ruse to keep her confined to the cave.

The birds flew and flew and came across a river where they saw some men panning for gems using huge bamboo troughs. They perched on a branch and watched as the men put their gems in a leather bag. There were dozens of beautiful sapphires, emeralds and rubies dazzling in the morning sun. The cranes stole some gems, hid them in their beaks and flew away.

Meanwhile, Biso was cooking lunch. The cat was hungry and was twirling around her legs. She chased it away. The cat got angry and urinated on the hearth, putting out the fire.

The meal had to be cooked before the cranes came home and she went out to find some fire. Soon, she was lost and found herself in front of *Rakshi's* cave.

Biso's beauty made the she-devil's daughter jealous and tried to keep her till her mother arrived. The little *Rakshi* told the girl that she would give her fire only if she cooked lunch for 20 people, because her mother's appetite was such that she needed that quantity at one sitting. Although it was hard work, Biso cooked the food before *Rakshi* arrived and the little she-devil gave her live coals in a coconut shell with a hole in it.

The coal ash dropped through the hole all along her way to the home cave. When *Rakshi* returned, her daughter told about the girl and asked her to follow the trail of ashes to reach the girl.

Rakshi went to the cave and asked Biso to open the door, imitating the mother crane's voice.

"Biso, Biso, open the door. I am your mother crane who has brought beautiful gems to string a necklace to enhance your good looks. Open the door, my lovely Biso."

The dog and the parrot were playing outside and they warned Biso not to come out and that it was the *Rakshi* who was talking like the crane. The she-devil got angry with the two creatures and killed them. After that she fixed a thumbnail in the upper door frame and a toenail on the threshold to kill the girl whenever she came out.

When the cranes returned, the girl came out to open the door and the she-devil's thumbnail pierced her head while the toenail pricked her foot. Biso was soon losing blood and fell unconscious.

The cranes removed the nails and the girl recovered. They tied the necklace made of blue sapphires, rubies and emeralds around her neck and asked her to go away.

"You have grown up and we are not able to look after you anymore", they told her. "Wear the same blood-splattered dress which will hide your beauty and protect you from evil people." The girl left the cave crying.

While walking through the woods she met the *Rakshi* and she offered herself as food. The she-devil said: "I don't want to eat a blood-soaked girl like you. I am looking for a beautiful princess who will be tastier than you."

Biso reached the king's palace and found employment as a kitchen helper. She used to remove her blood-covered cloth only when she went out to bathe in the river. A man, who was on a *kitul** tree tapping palm wine, saw her and told the king about a celestial being frolicking in the river.

The king who was looking for a consort, summoned Biso to his court and asked her to remove the blood-covered dress. She removed the dirty cloth, stunning everybody in the royal court with her remarkable beauty. The king was mesmerized by her and the story she narrated about her life.

He immediately announced a royal wedding, made Biso his queen and they lived happily, with several children and grandchildren until a ripe old age. They also had a menagerie of animals, which the people of the kingdom loved, and also a pond where cranes could come and go as they wished.

Story VII

Gamarala's Son-in-Law From The Netherworld

One day, when the Gama Mahage was combing her hair while seated in the veranda of her home, a man with a haggard appearance gingerly stepped into the compound and sat on the doorstep.

"Who are you? Are you looking for someone?", asked the woman looking curiously at the uninvited guest.

"*Elowa gihin Melowa Awa.*"* (I went to the Netherworld and came back)," the man said wiping sweat from his chest with a corner of the frayed *lungi* (sarong) he was wearing.

> (This is a widely-used idiom in Sri Lanka to describe recovery from a serious illness that could have cost one's life. Sri Lankans often use such colourful idioms in their conversations.)

"Is it true? When did you come from the other world?' the Gama Mahage asked, open-mouthed and supporting her cheek in both her hands.

"Only yesterday...," the man said and stopped, feigning a cough. He wanted to tell her that he came out of the hospital on the previous day but he did not add that part because he sensed that the chance encounter with the foolish woman might lead to a monetary windfall.

"You don't look that well. You look like a scorched cobra pulled out of an ant hill," the Gama Mahage said taking a close look at man's shrunken stomach and body bent like a creeper.

"I haven't eaten for days," he said squeezing the folds of his tummy as if to display the emptiness within.

"Don't people in the other world have food?"

"There are problems in the other world now. There has been a great famine over the last several years and the King of the Netherworld asked me to come to this world and see whether there is any way to take food from here," he said, his mouth watering as the smell of food being cooked in the kitchen wafted into the room.

"By any chance, did you happen to see my daughter Menika who died last year?" the woman asked.

The man saw a picture of a woman hanging on the wall.

"Menika...oh yes...There are many Menikas there. Is it the girl with a scar on the right cheek?"

"That is exactly right. Is she doing all right there?"

"Yes, yes. In fact, I married her a few months ago and she is expecting a child."

The woman jumped from the chair.

"Why are you sitting like a low-caste man on the floor? Get up, get up and sit on that ebony couch, my dear son-in-law."

The Gama Mahage asked the servant woman to hurry up and prepare lunch.

Without any invitation from the Gamarala's wife, he sat at the dining table and began to eat while the woman, who was saddened by the way he gobbled food, served him more rice, curry and other dishes.

"When are you going to the other world?" the woman asked after the man finished eating and burping after several extra helpings of buffalo curd and coconut treacle*. "You can rest here today so that you can meet the Gamarala when he returns from the fields."

"I have to go this evening, my dear mother-in-law. I never leave Menika alone even for a single night"

"What a nice son-in-law! So my daughter too has no food to eat there?"

"No, my mother-in-law. She, like all other people there, is starving."

The woman wiped her tears from the corner of her dress and asked the servant to pack some food.

"Does she have any jewellery there?"

"No, my mother-in-law. Gold is very expensive. In fact, she asked me to get her jewellery from her home."

"How can I be happy and live here when my only daughter is suffering there?" The Gama Mahage dragged a wooden chest from a room and put her daughter's jewellery into a reed bag and gave it to the man.

"Here, you can take my jewellery too." She removed her rings, gold necklace and the bracelets she was wearing and gave them to the man.

"How will you be travelling to the other world?"

The man looked around and saw a well-fed horse tied to the jack fruit tree* in the front yard.

"I rode the winds and the clouds on a heavenly horse, but it died on the way as it was starving."

"It doesn't matter anymore. Take our horse and go as fast as you can. However, next time you must come here with my daughter."

"I will definitely bring her along, my dear mother-in-law," the man said, taking the box of jewellery and the food parcel and hurrying to where the horse was. As the man was climbing onto the horse, the Gamarala returned from the paddy field.

The woman ran to her husband and said, "That is our son-in-law from the other world," and explained everything about her daughter and her 'husband'.

The Gamarala flew into a rage and beat his wife with his walking stick and ran after the man, who was already galloping away into the horizon, yelling: "Listen my son-in-law, when you ever come here again, take my foolish wife also to the other world."

Story VIII

Gamarala's Donkey Minds The Dog's Business

The popular Sinhala idiom *"Like donkey doing the dog's job"* means that someone is trying to make a fool of himself by trying to do someone else's job. The proverb comes from this Gamarala story.

A rich Gamarala had a dog and a donkey. The dog's duty was to guard the house in the night and during the day it accompanied its master to his paddy and vegetable cultivations on the outskirts of the village.

The donkey's duties were more strenuous than that of the dog. It was the beast of burden that carried the Gamarala's produce to the Sunday farmers' market and lugged the weekly supplies back to the house.

One rainy night, when the temperature had dipped below normal, the Gamarala's family went to bed early, snuggling under warm blankets. The dog fell into a deep sleep, curled up on a rug on the veranda.

The donkey was very tired after its trip to the market and was in its stable. It was, however, unable to sleep because of the pitter-patter of the rain on the stable roof.

It was a moonless night and some thieves, taking advantage of the bad weather, came to burgle the Gamarala's house. The men started removing the bricks on the outer wall to crawl into the house.

The donkey saw what the men were up to, but kept quiet as it thought the dog would bark to drive the thieves away. But nothing happened. The dog was fast asleep.

The donkey, although considered a foolish animal throughout history, felt sorry for his master.

"What would happen if these men steal the master's gold and silver? Won't he be a poor man without money even to feed me?" thought the donkey.

It began to bray loudly to warn the Gamarala about the intruders and the thieves fled.

The Gamarala, who awoke from an uneasy sleep, decided it was the donkey's braying that was causing his insomnia on that cold night. He went out with a flaming torch and walked around the house, but did not see anything unusual. The dog was curled up in the veranda, fast asleep.

"You foolish donkey! Why are you making such a noise, waking up the household in the dead of the night without letting us sleep after a hard day's work?" the Gamarala screamed.

He picked up a stick, went to the stable where the donkey was lying down and began to beat it. The donkey bore the pain stoically, and decided it would never do the dog's work again.

The next night, when the robbers came to the house again, the donkey kept quiet. It watched with sorrow as the gang carted away sacks of valuables. In the morning, the Gamarala's family woke up and realized what had happened. The Gamarala thrashed the lazy dog and chased it out of the house.

Story IX

Gamarala's Daughter And The King's Ring

After the Gamarala's wife died, he married a woman who had a daughter. The daughter of the new wife (the Gama Mahage) started living with Gamarala's own daughter in the adjoining house.

Meanwhile, the king was in the habit of visiting the Gamarala's daughter every night. The new Gama Mahage's daughter was jealous of the royal visit and complained to her mother.

"Daughter, stay awake tonight and tell me if the king comes again," she said.

The king visited the Gamarala's daughter again that night. The Gama Mahage then cut her toenail* the next evening and said: "My little one, bury this on the doorstep and cover it with dust."

The girl did as she was told.

That night, when the king stepped into the house the nail pricked his foot. Annoyed, he returned to his palace on his elephant and decided not to visit the house anymore.

The Gamarala's daughter couldn't stop crying. Some crows that were feasting on ripe jack fruit nearby felt sad and wanted to know why she was shedding tears.

"Oh *Kaputo* (crow), the king used to come and see me every night. He was injured by a toenail planted by the new Gama Mahage on the doorstep and he has stopped coming to visit me. That is why I am crying."

"Don't worry, little princess," one crow said. "A virgin must kill a flying crow with an arrow and extract its fat and apply it on the wound. This is the ideal medicine for such an injury."

The girl made a bow and an arrow with bamboo splits and coconut coir and shot a flying crow, extracted its fat and went to the palace disguised as a man.

The girl went to the king and said that she could heal him. Frustrated with many unsuccessful attempts by reputed physicians in the land, he allowed 'the man' to try his medication as a last resort.

'What will you give me if I heal you, My Lord?" asked the girl.

"I will give you a valuable ring made of pure gold," the king said.

The king was healed after the girl applied crow fat on his foot and extracted the toenail. As promised, the king gave her a gold ring.

After the foot was healed, the king decided to punish the person who caused the injury. He got onto his elephant and reached the home of the Gamarala's daughter. The king dragged the girl out by her hair and drew his sword to behead her.

She screamed. "Please don't kill me. I am the person who healed you."

The king lowered his sword and asked her to explain how she had healed him.

"I dressed up as a man and came to your palace, Your Highness, applied the crow fat as prescribed by some birds from heaven and took out the nail," the girl said.

"What did I give you for healing me?" asked the king, still holding the girl by her hair.

"Here is the gold ring you gave me," the Gamarala's daughter said, taking the ring from the folds of her dress.

The king was pleased with her reply and took the girl to the palace on his elephant and made her his queen.

Story X

The Gamarala's Gift

It was a golden summer one year and a village farmer found that a *ran kekiri** (a variety of gourd known as golden melon due to its colour, rarity and sweetness) was growing in his vegetable garden.

The farmer wanted to present the first fruit of the crop to someone of importance, and thought 'Who's better than Gamarala?"

The Gamarala was a friendly person who often came to his fields and garden inquiring about his work and advising him on increasing crop yields. He was also the first to visit with gifts when a birth occurred and the first to offer condolences to families in the village when someone died. He visited the sick and offered advice, based on his wide knowledge of *Ayurveda**.

The Gamarala also offered his cart pulled by two sturdy bulls when villagers needed to travel several miles into town for emergencies like a visiting a doctor or to buy jewellery and fancy goods.

The farmer plucked the *ran kekiri* and went to the Gamarala's house and presented the fruit. "This is the virgin fruit of my garden. Please accept this as a token of my affection," the farmer bowed and told the Gamarala.

The Gamarala was deeply touched by the farmer's gesture and accepted the gift. He wanted to acknowledge the farmer's humility and generosity and presented him with a pregnant cow.

"You have given me the best gift you can afford and in appreciation of your gesture I am giving you the best I can offer. This animal will be very useful to you," said the Gamarala handing over the cow.

The farmer at first refused to accept the gift, as a cow was a far too generous present in return for a *ran kekiri*, but the Gamarala insisted he takes the animal away. "The cow will give birth to a healthy calf and you can earn money by selling its milk."

The man was taking the cow home and on the way he met another villager who was squatting on a forest path with his hands on his chin. This villager was known as a lazy layabout who abhorred work and was always looking for handouts from people.

When he heard the story of the *ran kekiri* and the cow, he shivered with envy. "I will also go and give a gift to the Gamarala, something more valuable than a *ran kekiri*", the man thought. "In return, the Gamarala will give me a plot of land or a gold sovereign which I could sell off and live comfortably for some time." He had heard many stories from villagers about the Gamarala's generosity.

Next morning, the lazy farmer went to the Gamarala's house taking the only cow he had. Before leaving his house, he blamed his wife for his misfortunes and said his life was going to change for the better.

The wife, who tended to her paddy field without any support from the husband, protested against giving the cow as a gift since it was the only asset they had.

The Gamarala was puzzled by the appearance of the man at his doorstep so early in the morning, holding the rope tied around the neck of a cow.

"I am surprised to see you in the early morning. Villagers tell me that you sleep till the sun warms your backside! What brought you here early morning. Is your cow sick?" asked the Gamarala clearing his throat. The villagers consulted Gamarala for treating their sick cattle and goats.

"Oh no, this cow is quite healthy. I want to present it to you dear Gamarala because you are so helpful to us villagers. What better present than a cow!" said the farmer.

The Gamarala read the situation very well. He asked the villager to sit down and chew some betel leaves and inquired about his family.

"I should reciprocate your kind gesture," the Gamarala said, going into the house. After some time, he came back with a bag and presented it to the farmer.

"What better present than a rare, golden melon," said the Gamarala presenting him with the *ran kekiri.*

The villager went home with the bag. His wife was waiting for the expensive gift that she thought the Gamarala would give her husband. The man did not say a word as he placed the bag on a table. The wife peeped into it and all she saw was a *ran kekiri.*

"This is all he gave you?" blurted the wife.

He did not reply.

"Why did I take this lazy, foolish man as my husband? What sin did I commit in my past birth to marry an idiot like you? I could have carved a better one from a coconut branch! Now, how are we going to survive without the cow? I am going to my parents' home. They willl look after me."

She took the *ran kekiri,* smashed it on the ground and left the house forever.

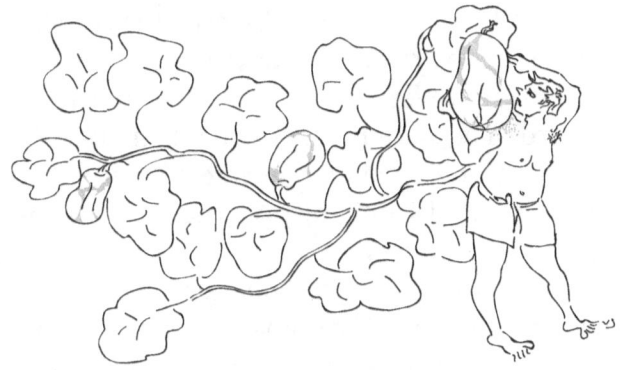

Story XI

The Gamarala And The Pumpkin Thief

A hard-working farmer lived in a village which was in the grip of a severe drought. Every morning, he trudged a couple of miles to a lake to get water for his vegetable garden.

The other farmers of the village did not want to toil. They spent their time cursing the weather, surviving on whatever food they could gather from the nearby forest.

The farmer's vegetable plot thrived and one day he was surprised to see an ash pumpkin plant sprouting a fruit. He dug a pit and hid it and spread dry leaves and earth to conceal it from the villagers.

Every morning and evening, he watered the plant and spent the night in a watch hut to chase away wild animals foraging for food.

One day, a villager who was hunting for food happened to pass the farmer's cultivation. He was surprised to find the pumpkin creeper still thriving despite the drought. On closer examination, he detected the young pumpkin hidden under a pile of dead leaves. By pressing the skin of the fruit he guessed the number of days it would take to ripen.

One night, however, the farmer could not keep watch over his garden because his wife had taken ill.

The next morning, when he came to the plot to water the plant, he found to his dismay that the pumpkin was missing.

The farmer went to the Gamarala's house and complained about the theft. The Gamarala felt sorry for the loss as he knew of the hard work put in by the farmer despite the ferocity of the drought.

The Gamarala sent out messages to all the villagers asking every one to come to his house as soon as possible.

The men gathered in the compound wondering about the early morning summons.

The Gamarala announced the theft of the ash pumpkin and asked the guilty person to confess and apologize to the farmer to avoid social embarrassment and boycott. Nobody came forward and all the villagers looked at each other and shook their heads.

Then Gamarala went around inspecting the shoulders of all the men and detected the presence of ash on one man's shoulder.

The Gamarala laughed out aloud, pointing his finger at the man. "A pumpkin thief is always known by the smear of ash on his shoulders."

The embarrassed thief apologized profusely and returned the pumpkin to its owner.

Story XII

The Gamarala And The Cow With Three Legs

One day, a village trader was taking a walk through a meadow and saw a bull belonging to the Gamarala mating with a three-legged cow.

A sudden thought flashed through his scheming mind. He looked around to ensure that no one else had seen the animals frolicking on the meadow. The trader thought he would be able to buy the three-legged creature at a low price as a crippled cow was of little value to a farmer.

He thought if he could convince the Gamarala to sell the cow he would also have a calf soon. He could keep the milch cow till it ran out of milk and sell it to the town butcher who came scouring the region once a week with his assistants to buy cattle for slaughter.

The man went to meet the Gamarala, who was seated on the veranda in a relaxed mood, munching betel leaves and smoking a Jaffna cigar*. The trader was offered some betel leaves and the Gamarala pushed the brass spittoon towards him.

The trader made small talk about the season's cultivation and how the late monsoon would affect the various crops. He then broached the subject of the three-legged cow. "Does that disabled cow belong to you, Gamarala?"

"Oh yes. I am very sorry that it lost one of its legs because of my own foolishness."

The visitor expressed surprise. "Your foolishness?"

The Gamarala said he was trying to shoot a wild boar in the jungle one evening. The animal, however, sprinted into the thick undergrowth with its many cubs.

The Gamarala caught a movement of a black object from the corner of his left eye and he was sure that it was the boar. He fired the gun in that direction and heard an animal cry and fall with a thud. It was his cow Raththi - Red - the name it inherited on account of a circular red mark in the centre of its forehead. The Gamarala couldn't understand how the cow had strayed into the jungle.

He was now reluctant to sell the cow, adding that his wife intended to look after the animal until its death. "It is our responsibility to the poor animal."

The trader strained his neck, trying to look into the house and inquired about the Gama Mahage. "Oh, she has gone to the river to take a bath," said the Gamarala.

The Gamarala's fondness for money and his foolishness were not a secret in the village. It was his shrewd, miserly wife, the Gama Mahage, who managed his lands and conducted financial dealings like paying the workers and selling the produce.

"How much will you charge if I want to buy that miserable three-legged animal?" the trader asked.

"I am not going to sell it without my wife's permission. She treats it like her own child."

"She is not here now. I will give you 100 rupees," said the man squinting his eyes and gazing down the road to see whether she was on her way home. "You can tell her that the cow must have wandered into the jungle once more. Any cow straying into the undergrowth will definitely be dinner for a leopard or two."

The Gamarala scratched his head.

"Why are you so interested in a three-legged cow?" asked the Gamarala, unable to understand why the man was offering him so much money for a cow which had only three legs. The previous month, the butcher had offered 10 rupees for the cow but the Gama Mahage had angrily said that it would be a *karmic* sin to sell an animal that had helped the family.

"It has been with us for so many years and helped us a lot when it was healthy. How can I be cruel to such a noble animal?" she told the butcher.

The trader explained he was under the influence of a malevolent planet and the temple priest had asked him to release a handicapped cow or a bull into the temple grounds to please the gods.

"The astrological positions of my star at this time of my life worry me a lot, Gamarala. They have ruined my business, my wife has run away with another man and taken my children with her and the priest told me I might even go insane."

The Gamarala felt sorry for the man's plight and accepted the 100 rupees.

"Hurry up and take the animal away before my wife returns from the river," the Gamarala told the man as he tucked the money in the knot of his sarong.

The Gamarala told about the sale of the cow to the Gama Mahage when she returned home. She exploded, letting out a string of curses on the Gamarala but wondered aloud which foolish man would pay that kind of big money for an old, barren and useless three-legged cow.

Story XIII

The Gamarala And
The Foolish Leopard

The Gamarala and his son rounded up their cattle late one evening and led the animals to their log enclosure.

The Gamarala asked his son to fasten the gate well, warning: "If you don't tighten the entrance the *"Kotiyo-Botiyo"* will come in the night and eat our cattle."

(Sri Lanka only has leopards and there is no historical evidence of the existence of tigers. Though the Sinhala word for the leopard is *diviya*, people generally use the term *kotiya* (tiger). Sri Lankans have the habit of making meaningless additions to words to make them rhyme, hence *Kotiyo-Botiyo*. *Kotiyo* is the plural of *kotiya*).

A leopard, which was slinking by, heard the word *botiyo* and thought the farmer was referring to some other animal. "What is this *botiyo* that they are talking about? Is it an animal bigger and stronger than me if it can snatch cows?"

The leopard was scared at the thought that the *botiyo* would come at any moment, so it entered the enclosure and hid among the cows.

A cattle thief entered the pen in the night and went around examining the cows to find the heaviest one. In the darkness, he felt the silky skin of an animal and he was certain that it was the heaviest and healthiest in the herd. The man hoisted the beast onto his shoulders.

The leopard thought it was a *botiyo* that had lifted him and stayed still, scared that it would be killed it if it tried to escape. The thief walked a long distance till morning broke through the trees. He was petrified to know that he had been carrying a leopard the whole night. The man ran up to a Buddhist temple that was built on a hill, threw the leopard down a precipice and escaped into the temple.

The injured leopard climbed back and began running to the temple to kill the man. On the way, it met a pregnant vixen that was nursing a craving for leopard meat.

"How did you get hurt like this, sir?" the jackal asked the leopard, prostrating before it. The leopard told the vixen about the incidents of the night and asked if there was a way to enter the temple.

"It is very simple, sir. Insert your tail through the hole like a key and it will open," the vixen said.

The leopard did what the cunning vixen asked it to do. When the leopard's tail came through the keyhole, the cattle thief grabbed it with all his might, knowing that someone passing by would kill the beast.

The vixen ran to the paddy fields and told the farmers about the trapped leopard. "This is a good chance to get rid of the beast that has killed so many of our cattle," said the Gamarala, who rushed to the temple with other farmers and killed the leopard.

The Gamarala skinned the animal and took away the pelt as a trophy, while the vixen called its kith and kin and feasted on leopard meat. The thief fled, never to return.

Story XIV

The Gamarala Finds A Son-In-Law With A 'Thuththiri' Tree

A rich Gamarala wanted to find a good husband for his young and beautiful daughter and sent messages to friends and relatives living in other villages inquiring about eligible bachelors.

Many men, who heard about the Gamarala's wealth and the beauty of his only daughter, started visiting the house as suitors.

The Gamarala wanted all the men to answer a simple question. "How will you destroy a grass burr growing in my garden?" (This kind of grass is known as *'thuththiri tree'* in the Sinhala language.)

The first to pay a visit was a doctor carrying his leather bag. The Gamarala invited the man to his house and asked his daughter to serve tea. This is the usual practice in Sri Lanka when a suitor pays his first visit to a girl's home. The doctor sat on a chair and the woman brought tea and some sweets on a tray. The act of serving tea to the man also gave him an opportunity to assess her beauty and health. The doctor was struck by her charm but was perplexed when the Gamarala asked him about the *'thuththiri tree'*.

"Isn't this man trying to demean my qualifications and my profession?" he thought. However, he said aloud, "Oh that's a very simple operation."

He opened his bag and pulled out a knife and a pair of scissors. "This is no big deal. I can cut it with either of these instruments," he said.

The Gamarala said, "My dear man, you are not qualified to marry my daughter."

The doctor was stunned by the refusal and left, thinking the Gamarala was out of his mind.

The next to arrive was a shabbily dressed professor with a pair of thick glasses hiding his intelligent eyes.

The girl served him tea and the professor was very happy with her composure and dignity. When the Gamarala asked him about the *'thuthiri tree'*, he replied, "There is no need of cutting it down. It is very simple. I can use a powerful herbicide to kill it instantly. It will also destroy all the weeds in your garden."

The Gamarala sent him on his way.

The next suitor was an accountant. The girl served him tea. He was taken up by her attention to detail and dexterity, in addition to her charming smile.

The Gamarala asked about cutting down the *'thuththiri tree'*. The accountant laughed nervously, hiding his irritation at being asked a question irrelevant to the subject of marriage or his qualifications. "I can pluck it with these," he said raising two fingers of his hand.

The Gamarala was not satisfied with his answer. One by one, several other educated and successful men were rejected as a future son-in-law by the Gamarala.

The sun was now setting when a man dressed in a simple

sarong and a shirt came to Gamarala's house. The young woman served him tea and he was impressed with her sturdy and brisk nature, a quality of a good housewife.

When the Gamarala asked him about cutting down the *'thuthiri tree'*, he immediately pulled up the sleeves of his shirt, took hold of the bottom ends of his sarong and tied them above his knees to make for easy movements. He spat into his hands, rubbed them together and said: "Now, give me an axe."

The Gamarala was pleased with his reply and selected him as his son-in-law. "At last, we have found a real man who is willing to do some real work," he told his wife.

PART II

Andare Stories

Andare, like the Gamarala, is a popular character in Sri Lankan folk tales. A court jester by profession, Andare was given the unique privilege of free access to the Royal Court at any time of the day, leading to hilarious situations.

According to oral history and a movie made about him in the early 1960s, Andare lived in the deep south of the island during the Portuguese era, beginning in the early 16th century.

Andare is believed to be a corrupt version of the name Andreas. There are historical records to show that court jesters existed in ancient Sri Lankan kingdoms. His responsibility was to entertain the king and his courtiers and help lighten the royal burden of governance.

Story I

How Andare Ate
The King's Sugar

Court jester Andare's craving for sweets was legendary and the king always ordered his chefs to make oil cakes, *aggala, kokis, helapa** and other traditional Sri Lankan sweets to keep him happy.

One day, Andare was passing the royal compound and he saw a large quantity of sugar spread on a mat.

He stood looking at the sugar for a long time, smelling its mildly intoxicating odour, and thought of a way to eat some of it, at the same time providing some entertainment to the king who had been worried by the news of a rebellion against him.

Andare went home and told his wife about the sugar in the royal compound and his craving.

"The king won't allow anybody to eat that sugar because it was a gift to the palace from the farmers," the wife said. "He will get very angry if you eat that."

Andare addressed his son. "I have a plan. The king is not in a good mood these days and I have to play a practical joke to make him laugh and forget his royal worries, and also get an opportunity to get a taste of that wonderful sugar," he said.

He took his son to another room and spoke to him so that his wife wouldn't hear their conversation.

"Son, tomorrow as soon as the sun is in the middle of the sky, run to the palace and shout that your mother has passed away."

The son didn't like that plan. "Isn't it bad to tell a lie like that? How hurt will my mother be if she knows what we are talking about."

Andare shrugged off his son's objections. "I am the court jester and my job is to make our king laugh to forget his worries. One day you might take my job and you have to learn the tricks of the trade."

The son agreed.

Next day, the son waited till he couldn't see his shadow on the ground, which meant that it was high noon, and ran to the palace.

Andare was at the Royal Court talking to the king and his advisors. They heard someone crying loudly and entering the assembly hall, "Father, oh my father, my dear mother and your dear wife has just passed away."

Everybody in the court rose, including the king, queen and the advisers. Andare embraced his son, ran out with him to the sugar mat and started rolling in the sugar. "Oh son, is there any use of our lives now? There is earth in your mouth and earth in my mouth," Andare cried eating handfuls of sugar while rolling on the mat, at the same time putting sugar in his son's mouth too. The king and his entourage watched helplessly.

*('Earth in a mouth' is an expression used by the
Sinhalese when a loved one or a breadwinner of a
family dies. This is an expression of grief meaning that*

everyone in the family is symbolically buried with the deceased).

The king sent his soldiers to Andare's house to inquire into the unexpected death.

Andare's wife ran to the palace after hearing about the prank.

The king and queen watched in amazement as the woman walked to the mat on which her husband and son were rolling, eating sugar.

Andare began to laugh loudly. The king realized this was another practical joke that his jester had planned to entertain him. He ordered his chefs to take all the sugar on the mat and make sweets for Andare's family.

Story ll

How Andare Lifted A Giant Rock

There was a big rock near the palace and the king considered it a security risk as it blocked the view of the many access points to the palace.

The king wanted it removed and he consulted many royal carpenters, masons and craftsmen, seeking their advice on how to move the rock away from the palace environs.

However, nobody had an answer to the vexed question. A thousand men or a thousand horses or oxen would not be able to pull the massive boulder out from the ground and move it away. One day, the king asked Andare whether he could do anything about it.

"Oh, that's a very simple job, my Lord," replied Andare.

The king was taken aback. "How can you do that?"

Andare laughed and said, "Feed me for one week with good food and I will remove it on the eighth day."

The king ordered that a special room be allotted to Andare in his palace and ordered the chefs to feed him with whatever food he desired. Andare feasted on varied and rich royal fare for seven days. On the morning of the eighth day, just as the dawn broke, Andare walked into the royal compound. The king, his officials and people gathered around the rock to see how Andare was going to remove it from the ground, knowing very well that breaking a promise made to the king was punishable by death.

Andare seemed calm. He went around the rock touching it as if he was trying to gauge its weight and meticulously measured the distance between his shoulders and the rock with his hands. He greased his palms with spittle, passed his rolled sarong between his legs and tied the ends behind the back into an 'amude' (loin-cloth).

He turned towards the crowd, hunched his shoulders and said; "Can someone lift this rock and place it on my back. I will carry it away to any place His Majesty orders me to take it."

Story III

How Andare Made The Ministers 'Lay Eggs'

After being the victims of Andare's pranks for many years, the ministers in the kingdom wanted to play a practical joke on the famous jester.

One day, when the royal entourage went for a bath at the palace pond, all the ministers, without Andare's knowledge, placed eggs at the muddy bottom.

The king, who knew the ministers' plan in advance, and also wanted Andare to be the target of a prank, asked: "Who among you can fetch eggs from the bottom of this pond?".

"Yes, we can," said the ministers, each of them diving headlong into the pond. Andare, clueless of what was going on, also jumped into the water.

All the ministers came up, triumphantly holding up an egg each and shouting "Here, here!" Andare also came up but he had no egg to show the king. He knew that he had been tricked by the royal party.

He laughed, cried like a rooster and said, "You are all hens and I am the only cockerel! I produced the eggs!"

Story IV

Andare Makes His Wife And The Queen Play Deaf

Andare had just married a girl from the deep south of the island and the talk in the kingdom was that the jester's wife was a very beautiful woman.

One day, the Queen summoned Andare to an audience with her and asked him to bring his wife to the palace. "I would like to meet your wife, Andare. Please bring her here. People say she is a very pretty woman."

Andare thought for a while. "Yes, Your Highness, people say she is beautiful, but I must admit that there is a little problem with her hearing."

The Queen smiled and asked him not to be concerned about his wife's disability. "I will talk loudly to her so that she will have no problem in understanding what I say."

Andare promised to bring his wife to the palace the next day.

He went home and told his wife about the Queen's invitation, but warned her that the queen was deaf. "Her world is mostly a world of silence, so you must talk to Her Royal

Highness as loud as you can."

Andare's wife felt great anguish that such a powerful person as the queen had a problem with her hearing and said, "I will speak at the top of my voice so that she will be able to at least faintly hear or understand me."

The next evening, the king was taking his usual afternoon siesta when he was awakened by loud noises coming from the direction of the queen's chamber. He rushed there and saw the queen and another woman gesticulating and talking loudly with each other.

"What is this pandemonium? Who is this woman?" the king asked the queen, pointing towards Andare's wife.

"This is Andare's wife. She is a little dull of hearing and Andare asked me to speak to her loudly," the queen said.

Andare's wife felt as if she was shrinking with shame. She was afraid and started to cry. "Forgive me, My Lord. I am talking loudly because Andare told me that the queen is deaf." The king shook his head and began laughing.

Story V

How Andare Ate The King's Jambu Fruits

Andare had a great liking for *jambu** fruits and he was the first one to taste them from the tree in the royal garden every season. The king asked the jester several times to give the royalty the honour of tasting the fruits first but His Highness' request fell on deaf ears. The tree had a sentimental value for the ruler as it was a gift from an Indian king.

Once more the *jambu* tree in the courtyard was full of red, juicy fruits. Unable to wean Andare away from his greed for *jambu*, the king issued an order banning anyone from looking at or touching the fruits on the royal tree. Andare secretly admired the fruits glistening in the sun on branches bent with its bounty. He was planning to evade the royal decree and thought of a plan to enjoy the fruits.

One day, he asked his son to blindfold him and tie his hands behind his back. After that the jester went under the tree and ate all the fruits that reached his mouth as he walked around. He went on tiptoe and ate the fruits above and had his fill. He neither saw nor touched the branches.

The following morning, the king heard that a lot of the *jambu* fruits were missing. He ordered the guards to find the thief and bring him in for punishment. The soldiers, according to eye witnesses, caught the *jambu* thief and brought him before the court. The king was surprised to find that the man who defied his order was none other than his favourite jester. But according to law, a wrong doer must be punished. Andare pleaded innocence as he had eaten the fruits without seeing or touching them.

"Again you have defied my orders and ate the *jambu* fruits without letting me enjoy them first. I am going to punish you for your audacity. Do you have any excuses? How can you eat them without seeing or touching?" the king thundered.

"My Lord, we all know that your order was not to look at the fruits or touch them. You never asked not to eat the *jambus*," said Andare with a smile.

The king asked Andare to show how he ate the fruits. The jester had a hearty laugh, went under the tree, closed his eyes and opened and closed his mouth many times.

The king, the queen and the royal court were amused and started laughing.

Story VI

Andare And The Tapper

Andare was spending a few days in the village, when one morning he saw coconut trees being tapped for palm wine. What better than a drink of night-chilled coconut sap in the morning before it matures with the rising sun!

So, Andare sat in a coconut grove and saw a man soon arriving with a pot tied to his waist. The man ignored Andare and scampered up a coconut tree using coconut husks tied to the trunk like steps. The man climbed down and poured the toddy into a big pot. Andare asked whether he could get some of the toddy. The man said civet cats had drunk all the sap. He climbed up the next tree, came down and poured more into the pot. When he was climbing the third tree, Andare sang out:

"May the foot slip from every rung; May every string holding the rungs snap; May the tapping knife be tainted with blood; May the man who refuses to give me palm wine fall off the tree..."

The man felt a sudden chill as the song sounded like a curse and knew it was none other than Andare. He climbed down, placed the pot near the jester's feet, apologized profusely and said he would offer him wine every morning.

Story VII

Andare's Duel With A Giant

A belligerent giant walked into the kingdom one day. He went around the villages challenging people to fight him, and killed many with his bare hands. The giant was tall as a palm tree and had arms like iron bars. He emptied the clay silos and granaries of the farmers and slaughtered cattle to satisfy his voracious appetite.

Village chieftains from far-flung areas appealed to the king for help. The king summoned his advisors to discuss a plan of action. The palace had some big men in service but they were reluctant to face this terrible foreigner.

Finally, the giant reached the palace and bellowed outside the gates. The king sent a message saying that the kingdom's strongest warrior would fight him and offered him a special room in the palace.

The king then summoned Andare who laughed till his ribs stretched to breaking point.

"Are you sure you will fight him?" the king asked Andare looking at his body, which was thin like a reed.

"I have fought bigger giants," Andare said, preparing betel leaves and areca nuts. "Leave it to me, My Lord. But there are some arrangements to be made."

"I will give you anything you ask," said the king.

"Let me live adjoining the giant's room for 21 days and feed me the best food you can find. On the 21st day I will fight the giant," said Andare.

A room adjoining the giant's accommodation became Andare's quarters for 21 days and he feasted on royal fare.

One night, when the giant was sleeping Andare quietly removed the plaster on his side of the wall and a few bricks. He took care not to damage the wall on the giant's side.

A few days before the fight Andare asked the giant if he could get some betel leaves and areca nuts. "I have betel leaves but how can I pass them to you? There are no windows in the room," the giant replied.

"Don't worry. Just pass them to me through this hole," said Andare smashing his arm through the weak wall. The giant could not believe his eyes when Andare's hand extended through the shattered wall.

The giant shivered as he passed the betel leaves.

The day of the epic duel arrived. People gathered in their hundreds in the palace courtyard. One finger of the giant was bigger than one arm of Andare, people said.

Andare was brought into the yard accompanied by dancers and drummers. He was dressed only in his loincloth and his body was well oiled. He came, bowed before the king with a smile and raised his hands, turning around to accept the nervous applause of his countrymen.

The king ordered the soldiers to fetch the giant.

A few minutes elapsed before pandemonium broke out in the arena as the soldiers ran to the king shouting that the giant had disappeared. Many people said the giant was seen fleeing the kingdom at dawn.

The king praised Andare's fearlessness and presented him with gold bars equal to the weight of an elephant.

PART III

King Kekille Stories

King Kekille is another character that features prominently in Sri Lankan folk tales. He was famous for his outrageous and hilarious judgements which mostly saw the guilty party go scot-free and innocent people punished for crimes they never committed..

King Kekille is a potent symbol of the injustice that is visceral to absolute rule. The many Kekille stories represent attempts by the powerless of a bygone era to use humour (often of the gallows' variety) to highlight (and to come to terms with) the structural precariousness and insecurity of ordinary life in a lawless land under a ruler who dispenses arbitrary justice.

Story I

King Kekille And The Audacious Thief

One night a thief broke into King Kekille's palace but the alert guards caught the man and brought him before the king early in the morning.

King Kekille flew into a royal rage and berated the thief for his audacity to break into his regal quarters with the intention of stealing. The thief fell at the king's feet.

"Oh, Sire," pleaded the cunning thief. "It is not my fault, it's the fault of the mason who constructed the palace wall."

"How come?" thundered the king.

"My Lord, if the mason had built strong walls which cannot be scaled or broken, I could never have entered the palace. As Your Lord can see, he is the guilty party to this crime."

The king thought for a moment and then nodded in agreement.

The mason was rounded up by soldiers and brought in chains to the palace. The king said he needed an explanation for the shoddy construction of the wall that endangered the security of the royal household.

"My Lord, I am not guilty. It is my assistant who is responsible, as I feel he mixed too much sand with the cement," said the mason.

The royal brain was now considering several heavy questions. "How can I punish an innocent man?"

The soldiers were ordered to arrest the mason's assistant. The assistant trembled as he appeared before the king.

He said, "Oh My Lord, I was mixing cement with water when I was distracted by a buxom woman who was passing by the work site, swinging her colossal hips this way and that way."

The woman was summoned to the court. Indeed, the woman was voluptuous and far more attractive than the concubines in the king's harem.

The royal mind sighed and regretted not seeing this wonder of nature before he limited the number of his concubines with a royal decree designed to pacify the people who opposed his excesses.

"It is true My Lord! I was passing by this man while he was engaged in his work but it is not entirely my fault. My jeweller delayed making my ear-rings for a long time and that's why I had to make several visits to his shop, passing the man who was mixing cement," the woman said in a sing-song voice with a wiggle of her hip.

"Her voice is like a lullaby", the king thought, gesturing to two women of his harem who stood beside him to swing their feather fans briskly to keep him cool.

The king ordered the immediate arrest of the jeweller. He had had enough of the excuses and decided to put the matter to rest without further exercising his royal brain.

The goldsmith, who was thin like a creeper, was summoned to the court and sentenced to death without being given a chance to explain his innocence.

The man was to be killed by King Kekille's favourite method of punishment; he was to be tied to a tree and the royal tusker was to gore him to death.

The jeweller wailed, "Oh King, I am a very thin man and do not have enough flesh on my bones for the tusks to penetrate. Your favourite elephant might break its tusks by hitting the tree. I know a fat butcher in my village who is fit for this punishment."

King Kekille thought for a moment and ordered his soldiers to arrest the butcher.

The fat butcher, wearing blood-splattered clothes, appeared before the royal court.

The king agreed with the jeweller after seeing the well-rounded butcher and ordered that the royal tusker gore him to death for allowing a thief to break into the palace.

"He deserved it," the king declared and all the courtiers nodded their heads in agreement.

Story II

King Kekille's Deadly Morning Ritual

Some Sri Lankans, particularly in the rural areas, have the habit of blaming the first person they see in the morning if they have a bad day; quite similar to the idiom of 'getting up on the wrong side of the bed'.

Some believe that seeing a pregnant woman, a child, a person who is believed to be lucky, a woman with a pot of water or milk or an elephant can make for a great day.

King Kekille was no stranger when it came to this kind of superstitions. He ordered a person who was believed to be lucky in his country to stand near his window every morning. The man was paid handsomely for his duties that lasted only a few minutes every day.

He could have asked his mahout to be with the elephant near his window in the morning but the king did not like it as the beast was used for executing hardened criminals as part of carrying out his judgments.

One day the man fell ill and was unable to be present near the window. The king woke up early in the morning and when he opened the window, he saw a man, dressed in rags! The king let out a sigh, followed by a crude curse, knowing it was going to be a bad day. He went to the washroom and finished his morning ablutions, thinking of the unfortunate events he would have to face that day.

Next, it was the turn of the royal barber to shave the king's beard with a golden razor. While the barber was doing his job, the king let out a sneeze, making the man lose his grip, cutting a part of the royal nose. The king flew into a rage. The barber knelt down and pleaded innocence.

"Pardon me, My Lord. It was not my fault. It was your mighty sneeze that caused this unfortunate mishap," the barber stammered.

"It is not your fault, nor the fault of my sneeze. It is the fault of that *kalakanni* (unfortunate) scoundrel I saw this morning," King Kekille thundered. He ordered his soldiers to arrest the man who passed by the window.

A man dressed in the same rags was hauled into the courts and he explained that he was merely seeking alms to feed his family.

The king pointed at his injured nose and accused him of shedding royal blood. The man was sentenced to death and the court agreed with the king's decision.

That evening, the man was brought to the execution ground, accompanied by drummers and trumpeters as people gathered to witness the punishment.

The mahout was on the tusker's back barking commands and kicking the elephant below its ears, ordering the beast to gore the man. The man faced the king and spoke, "Oh King, you are the first man I saw this morning and that is why I am being killed. You only lost a part of your nose but I am losing my life, and my wife is losing her husband and my children their father."

King Kakille, however, did not retract his judgement.

PART IV

Maha Dena Muththa

Maha Dena Muththa (The Elder Who Knows Everything) is, like the Gamarala, a beloved character in Sri Lankan folk tales. He is portrayed as a flamboyant celebrity, who is consulted by the villagers whenever they face a difficult situation.

Maha Dena Muththa's judgments, although many times foolish or bordering on the ridiculous, are wonderful words of wisdom for the villagers who obey them out of blind devotion to the man. This 'wise man' has five disciples who are named according to their physical appearance, just like Snow White's seven dwarfs.

Indikatu Pancha, thin like a needle, is one of his pupils. Then, there is Polbe Moona, a man whose face looked like half of a split coconut.

Kotu Kitayya is thin as a stick, Puwak Badilla is lean and tall like an areca nut palm while the last one, Rabboda Aiya is a big man with a big belly. Maha Dena Muththa's disciples always accompany him on his missions.

Story I

The Wise Man And The Head of A Goat

One day a farmer rushed to the man who knows every-thing to find an answer to a serious problem.

His thirsty goat had tried to drink water from an earth-en pot and got its head stuck in it. The farmer's attempts to free the goat from the pot had proved futile, so he rushed to Maha Dena Muththa's house.

The wise man and his disciples accompanied the farmer to the farm. One pupil carried a heavy book on his shoul-ders in which Maha Dena Muththa had jotted down solu-tions to all kinds of worldly problems.

He inspected the goat and felt sorry for the animal's plight and asked the pupil to read from a page about goats in the book.

After listening to the pupil, Maha Dena Muththa asked the farmer to bring a knife, with which he beheaded the goat. "Now, you crush the pot and take its head out," said the man who knows everything. Problem solved!

Story II

Maha Dena Muththa In Search Of New Pupils

Maha Dena Muththa got up one morning with a raging urge - he wanted to impart his profound knowledge and years of wisdom to more people. He decided that he was getting old and there was not much time left for him in this mortal world.

"It is very important that more students gather around me to learn all the wonderful things I have in my head," he told his five obedient pupils.

"At the least, I must have a dozen pupils with me now. They will then be able to take all what they have learnt to every corner of the country."

His pupils nodded in agreement and promised to do all they could to bring more students. Maha Dena Muththa asked them to carry his famous book where he had recorded his past judgements and the many critical legal rules that could be applied to particular circumstances.

He led his posse, carrying his walking stick, which was a constant companion and represented his authority, and sometimes used as a weapon to protect his august self against an audacious thief, a cobra, or a monkey trying to get too friendly with him.

On the way, he spoke to many young men to test their general knowledge on philosophical subjects and jurisprudence, but no one seemed to have a suitable level of intelligence to be inducted into his inner circle. He loudly lamented the declining standards of education in the country and the lack of moral discipline.

Along with his diligent five pupils, Maha Dena Muththa walked through several villages until dusk fell and it was time to rest. "We will continue our search tomorrow," the wise one said. The men came across an '*ambalama*'*, a one-room resting place constructed on the wayside for weary travellers to spend the night.

They were feeling very hungry and Maha Dena Muththa asked his pupils to cook a satisfying dinner. He asked them to go to the nearby village to find suitable farm produce to prepare the food.

Maha Dena Muththa assigned each of his pupils to co-operate in the venture as he took a breather under a banyan tree. He asked one to find three bricks to make a hearth and ordered another to bring rice. Another one was asked to bring good vegetables. One was asked to bring some banana leaves to serve the meal while the fifth was asked to wait behind and get ready to cook, using the ingredients brought by the others.

The pupil who was ordered to bring rice returned empty-handed.

"Why, isn't there rice in this village? I see the fields stretching into the horizon, bristling with maturing rice," thundered Maha Dena Muththa, unable to control his hunger pangs.

"My Lord...the rice seller wanted more money for rice

and I decided not to buy at that exorbitant price," said the man. The wise one nodded and replied, "That's good. One should not waste money unnecessarily."

He saw the one who was assigned to find bricks to make the hearth come without bricks.

"What happened? Aren't there bricks in this village despite the large number of kilns we saw on the way?"

"Pardon me Sire...I couldn't find three bricks of the same size," said the pupil, his hands folded and with tears in his eyes.

"That's right. How can you keep a pot on an uneven hearth?" Maha Dena Muththa agreed.

He turned towards the one who was asked to bring vegetables. "You, what happened to the vegetables? Don't we see gardens everywhere with green vegetables?"

"Pardon me Sire....Here, the bitter gourds are too bitter. Okra is bad for phlegm and pumpkin is fattening. Why should we eat things that are bad for our health and fall sick? I could also not find any spices."

"Yes, that's true. If we fall ill, how can we go looking for more recruits tomorrow?" asked Maha Dena Muththa.

The last one who went in search of banana leaves also returned empty-handed. "You, what happened? Didn't we see enough banana cultivation in this part of the world?"

"Yes Sire, we saw a lot of banana trees but when I tried to cut a leaf, a *kirala** bird cried nearby. Isn't the *kirala* bird's cry a bad omen?"

"Yes, yes, indeed, my pupil! One should immediately stop all activities when a *kirala* bird cries. It is a very bad omen," said the Elder who Knew Everything, knowing that all of them had to starve that night.

Story III

How Maha Dena Muththa Found The Missing Man

Maha Dena Muththa and his five pupils went to the woods one day to cut sticks for a fence. They worked hard the whole day to cut and shape the sticks, which they bound together to make five strong bundles.

As evening fell, it was time for them to return home. Maha Dena Muththa began to count and found only five men among them. He was not counting himself.

All of them began to cry and started poking the river with long sticks thinking that one of them had drowned.

Maha Dena Muththa counted again and again and each time, the number stopped at five. They could not go home, leaving one of them behind. What could they tell the wife and the children of the missing one?

Once again they started crying and went deeper into the jungle to look for the missing one, thinking he could have got lost somewhere or had been attacked by an animal.

Finally, on one of the jungle paths, they found a villager returning home with his two buffaloes after grazing them on a nearby hill. "Oh villager, did you see a man wandering about in the jungle, or lying somewhere hurt or crying?"

The villager wanted to know more details. "When we set off from home there were six of us and when I count now there are only five," Maha Dena Muththa told the man. "One man is missing."

Dusk was falling and the man looked closely at Maha Dena Muththa and his pupils and recognized them. He knew that they had built a reputation in the region as fools.

The man asked Maha Dena Muththa to rearrange the wood on the ground, making a total of six bundles. The pupils followed the man's instructions. "Now each one of you take a bundle of wood and move away," he said. The man began counting loudly. "One...two...three...." as Maha Dena Muththa and the men picked up a bundle of wood each.

"Four...five...six. That accounts for all six of you."

Maha Dena Muththa thanked the man profusely and set off for home wondering how a villager who did not look very intelligent, brought the missing man back.

"Some kind of witchcraft," he muttered to himself.

Story IV

How Maha Dena Muththa Ended The Drought

Maha Dena Muththa's village was in the grip of a severe drought and the people were suffering. Finally, he decided to solve the problem and set out on a bullock cart with his faithful disciples. On the way they came across a well brimming with clean water. They drank water to their heart's content and even bathed and washed the bullock.

Maha Dena Muththa thought that if they could steal the well and take it to their village, it could end the drought. His disciples agreed to the plan and hailed his wisdom. So they waited until dark to remove the wall around the well.

After reaching their village, Maha Dena Muththa asked the villagers to gather in the square because he had found a solution to end the drought. Everybody gathered with pots and pans to collect water. Maha Dena Muththa asked his disciples to dig a hole and bury the well. They did so. He peered into the well hoping to see fresh water bubble up. He was sure everything went according to his brilliant plan but wondered aloud why there was no water in the well.

PART V

Rakshayas & Yakshayas

The Rakshayas and the Yakshayas are two popular characters featured in Sri Lankan folk tales.

They are supernatural ogres, visible or invisible to human eyes depending on the circumstances. The intended likenesses of the Rakshayas and Yakshayas are featured on Sri Lankan traditional masks and temple paintings, with bushy, tussled hair, eyes as large and red like *Goraka** fruits and two fangs protruding sideways from both sides of the mouth, and the body covered in thick hair.

The *shamans* (village wizards) are supposed to tame them by their magical powers to get certain things done or to harm their enemies or the people they despise. In Sri Lankan folk tales, these ogres can be friendly or hostile to human beings.

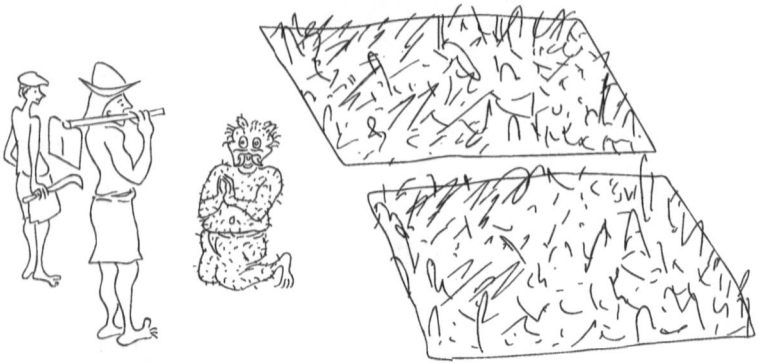

Story I

The Ogre, Some Magic And The King's Illness

There was once a *rakshaya* living on a drumstick tree (*Moringa oleifera**) opposite a house, intending to harm the people living there. In fact it was an ogre tamed by a *shaman* (village wizard) who had a grudge against them. It was bound by charms to reside in the tree waiting for a suitable opportunity to destroy the family.

One day the husband and son set out to work in their paddy fields. The woman of the house was trying to cut some vegetables for lunch and found the knife rusty and blunt. So she went near the drumstick tree and sharpened the knife on a stone. She felt both edges of the blade with her fingers to test its sharpness saying to herself, "Now I can cut even a *Rakshaya's* neck with this," and held it against the sun to see how the old rusty knife now glinted like a brand new one.

The ogre thought: "Oh, now the woman knows my presence here and she is trying to kill me. I must escape from here to save my life." He ran in the direction of where her husband and son were heading to and pleaded with them to save him from the woman.

The ogre fell at the feet of the husband, saying: "Your wife threatened to kill me and I will do anything for you if you can spare my life from her sharp knife."

The husband and the son were scared and wanted to run away, but they did not betray their nervousness before the ogre. They had heard that supernatural beings are afraid of fearless human beings.

"How can you help us?" asked the husband, standing erect and pretending to be tough.

"I will help both of you to become *shamans* and help you earn lot of money with my magical powers," the *Rakshaya* said.

So the father and son became *shamans* and went from village to village driving away evil spirits from people, healing mysterious illnesses, helping men to win the hearts of women and performing many other tricks.

The *Rakshaya* who remained invisible behind the two men when they performed rituals helped them with his powers. The father and son soon became wealthy and known throughout the land.

After many years the *Rakshaya* became bored and wanted to go away. When the ogre expressed his desire to leave, the man said he would ask the wife to kill him if he ever entertained the idea of deserting them.

The ogre left anyway and went to the palace and entered the body of the king, bringing His Royal Highness under his spell and making him sick.

The king, distressed because of his deteriorating health, promised gold equal to the weight of an elephant to any person who could heal him. Soldiers were sent around the country looking for healers and *shamans*. Many renowned doctors in the land and other countries came to the palace and tried to heal the king. All their efforts were in vain. While lying on his deathbed the king, who had heard about the exploits of the father and the son duo, ordered his soldiers to bring the *shamans* to his palace.

The men were, however, losing popularity and surviving on the money they earned in their heyday. Their magic had failed to yield any results after the *Rakshaya* had left them.

The soldiers located the two and brought them to the palace. The father and son walked into the royal court with drooping heads of dejected men. They knew that death awaited them if they failed to heal the royal body.

The two fell at the king's feet and begged for mercy saying that they had lost their powers because of unfavourable planetary transitions. The king thought that the father and son duo did not have the will to treat him for some reason beyond his knowledge. Meanwhile, the *Rakshaya* was enjoying the fun, making the king's health worsen, wanting to shame the two *shamans* and prove to the world that they were frauds.

The King spoke to the two, "Why don't you like to help me? Am I not your king who looks after you lovingly, providing your every need? I have a feeling that you don't like to treat me. May be you harbour some grudge against me. I will give you two days. If you fail to heal me I will kill you by placing both of you on steel spikes."

This ancient method of punishment was known as *ula thiyanawa* and was reserved for the king's worst enemies or those who rebelled against his reign. The wrongdoer was forced onto a spike which would slowly penetrate the body and then exit through the chest. It took several excruciating days for a man to die this way.

The father knew instinctively that it was the *Rakshaya* causing the royal sickness and they asked the king's permission to try one last treatment. The permission was granted. The men began their rituals, beating drums, chanting and burning incense. The father pretended to go into a trance and told his son loudly to bring his wife with her sharp knife to cut the *Rakshaya's* neck. The ogre panicked and hurriedly left the king's body.

The king, who instantly became his old bouncy self, presented them with gold equal to the weight of two elephants and sent them on their way.

Story II

The Broken Drum

Sri Lankans often embellish their conversations with idioms that cannot be easily translated into other languages. One of the idioms used to describe a futile effort is *Gahapu Bere Kuth Nehe, Bere Paluwakuth Nehe* (*The drum has lost one half though there was not much dancing to play for*). This idiom is based on the following folk tale:

Once upon a time, an elephant died in a jungle. A hungry fox began eating the cadaver, creating a hole on the side of the dead pachyderm. It later crept into the hole and started eating the meat in the interior. While it was busy inside, the hide dried out in the summer heat and caved in, imprisoning it inside the elephant's body.

A drummer, who was on his way to a *thovil* dance passed the dead elephant.

> *(Thovil is an all-night ritual accompanied by chanting, dancing and drumming to heal someone who is ill due to the influence of evil spirits. The idea is to expel the spirit from the body of the affected person.)*

The fox heard the drummer's footsteps and demanded to know who was passing by.

"I am going to a *thovil* ceremony," said the drummer.

"How dare you trespass into my territory without my permission?" thundered the fox.

As the drummer couldn't see anybody, he thought a *rakshaya* with a home in a nearby tree was talking to him. "Excuse me, sir," the man pleaded, looking around. "I was not aware that I should take permission from a *rakshaya* to pass through this area."

"What do you get when you play the drum at the '*thovil*'," asked the fox.

"I get food and some money."

"You are lucky to pass this way today," said the cunning fox. "I am a *rakshaya* guarding a treasure of gold here. I will tell you how to get all the gold under my protection if you do as I tell you."

The drummer agreed.

"I see that you have a drum. Break the hide on one side, fill the drum with water and pour it on this elephant."

People did not dare go against a *rakshaya's* orders and be a target of his wrath. The drummer broke the hide on one side of the drum, went to a nearby pond, filled the drum with water and poured it on the elephant's body several times. The smell was horrible, but the drummer was thinking of the gold he would get as a reward. The water made the hide soft and the fox got out of the maze of elephant bones and fled into the jungle.

The drummer looked everywhere inside the cadaver but did not see anything except maggots. He looked around and said: "I have done my duty. Now, can I please have my reward?" There was only the humming sound of the wind in the trees.

The man picked up his broken drum and went home, regretting his foolishness and lost income from the *thovil* dance.

Story III

Jack Fruit - Gift From God

When the Great Brahma created human beings, he gave them many kinds of fruit trees, but did not tell them which ones to eat.

Many died trying to eat poisonous ones and it took many years for man to select the good from the bad. But there was one tree, the fruits of which humans never dared to eat. It was the jack tree. The trees were huge and it was difficult to climb them and the fruits were the largest in the world. Nature encased them in prickly skins and they had a white sticky substance that oozed when cut.

When ripe, the whole area was heavy with its cloying aroma but humans left it alone thinking it was the food of the Rakshayas. The God of Gods, *Sakhra Deva*, was annoyed that people were not eating the fruits and one day came down to earth, disguised as an old man. He asked a woman to cook a young jack fruit for him. She found the broth had an irresistible aroma and told herself, "I must taste this, even if I die." Morsel by morsel, the woman finished the whole pot and nothing happened to her. From that day on, the jack fruit became the staple diet of many people.

PART VI

Animals & Birds

Fables about talking birds and animals exist in every culture and stories from *Aesop's Fables* and India's *Panchatantra** have regaled children and adults for generations. Bird and animal stories abound in Sri Lankan villages too and these are an essential element of rural conversation and some stories have been compressed to become popular proverbs.

Animals and birds are given human behavioural traits and talk and act just like humans in their interaction with villagers or their own kind. It is interesting to note the many similarities between animal stories in the Buddhist *Jataka* tales and the *Panchatantra*.

Story I

The Hermit Cat

A hungry cat was trying to steal food from a house. It pounced on a rice ball placed by the house-owner inside a small shrine, as an offering for his guardian deities.

The cat's neck, however, went through a rosary. To add to its misery, some of its whiskers got singed when its face went too close to a lamp as it tried to wriggle out.

He tried to sniff his way out and accidentally dipped his forehead into a saucer of mustard paste on the pedestal. As a result, a strip of yellow decorated his forehead.

After escaping from the house, the cat was disoriented and kept losing his balance. It couldn't pick up smells and knew he was in for some rough times ahead until the whiskers grew back.

The tomcat, however, knew that every bad event was followed by something favourable. He met a sparrow on the way. The bird was taking a sand bath on the road and tried to fly away when it saw the cat.

"Have no fear, my friend," the cat spoke to the bird. "I have become holy. Look at the rosary I am wearing. I am on my way to the jungle to become a hermit and meditate in a cave. I will never eat the meat of a living animal. Never again!"·

The sparrow looked at the cat and saw the rosary which was only worn by holy men living in the forest and also the strip of yellow mustard paste which only deeply religious people apply on their foreheads. There must be some truth in what the cat just said, thought the bird.

"I am going to the jungle to find a cave to meditate. Come and help me to find one."

The sparrow, impressed with the changed attitude of the cat, joined him and flew along overhead.

They met a hare on the way, which tried to run away. The sparrow explained how the cat had become holy and that there was nothing to fear. "I am accompanying the Cat Hermit to his cave to meditate. He has taken a vow never to eat the meat of a living animal. See how he is wearing a rosary and the yellow mustard paste on the forehead."

"Do I have mustard paste on my forehead?" The cat ran to the edge of a little pond to check his face. "How holy is that!" he exclaimed.

The hare wanted to impress the cat, which had earlier hunted and killed many of its cubs. "You do look saintly. I can run fast and find a good cave for you."

"There is no need to run, just walk with us," said the cat, licking his lips.

The three animals were sauntering down a forest path, when they met a mouse. The mouse was ready to run, but hesitated and looking at the strange trio - cat, sparrow and hare - wondered, "Is the world changing?"

"Hello my friend," the hare spoke to the mouse. "You don't have to worry any more about the cat. He has become holy and renounced his old ways. He is going to the jungle to meditate and we are now looking for a good cave. He has taken a vow never to eat the meat of a living creature."

The mouse trusted the hare. The cat looked different with the rosary and its colourful beads.

The cat suddenly decided that it wanted to rest under a tree. Even the monkeys on the tree were surprised by the cat wearing a holy rosary and a mark on the forehead.

The cat could not control its hunger anymore and suddenly pounced on the sparrow, tearing its throat apart. The sparrow did not have a chance even to squeak and died in the jaws of the cat.

"Is it a sin to eat a dead animal?' the cat asked the hare and the mouse.

"Definitely, it is not a sin," replied the two, now planning to make a fast getaway. They thought they would wait until the cat fell into a sleep.

"It is a sin only if you eat a living animal," said the hare.

The cat ate the sparrow.

Invigorated, the cat said he wanted to continue his journey to find a cave to meditate.

It was late evening when they reached the edge of the jungle, and the cat was now ravenous. It killed the mouse with one wild sweep of a paw and played with the carcass for a few minutes, turning and pushing it around. The cat asked the hare whether it was a sin to eat a dead animal.

"It is not at all a sin to eat a dead animal," said the hare.

After killing the mouse, the cat lunged towards the hare with its bloody claws fully stretched. The hare, which expected the attack, sprang over the cat and dashed into the jungle, shouting: "When did cats become holy? Oh, we are such fools!"

Story II

A Foolish Donkey Dies In Bid To Become King

The lion, the king of the jungle, was getting old. All his life he had lazily lounged about in his cave, letting his wife do the hunting and bring him food.

When the lion queen died, her sons eloped with other lionesses to distant jungles leaving their father to his fate.

The lion was now getting weaker. Several attempts to hunt even small animals like hare and mouse-deer were not successful. He lacked the tact and patience of his wife. His advancing age was also making his movements clumsy. The king, at last, was starving and his days seemed to be numbered.

One day, a jackal, which was passing by the lion's den heard him roar and peeped into the cave.

"Ayubowan* *(Wishing you a long life)*, Your Lordship! Are you healthy and well, Sir?" the jackal asked looking at the dark blob moving inside the cave.

The lion came out yawning. His once majestic cheeks were sunk like withered jack fruits and the wrinkled tummy hung loose, giving him the appearance of a mangy dog.

The lion had no liking for jackal meat, but they remained distant friends. The lion thought the jackal was mean and selfish. The jackal hung around the den to eat the remains of animals and quarrelled with other animals as if it was in the same power league as the King.

"I am old and weak," the lion said, making the jackal rejoice inwardly at the plight of the patriarch.

"I am starving," the lion said, kneeling down.

"Old age is common for all Sir...animals, human beings... I can help you. I can't chase deer or wild buffaloes but I can help you hunt something to fill your stomach," the jackal said, leaving the den, promising it would return soon.

He met a donkey grazing on dry grass.

"*Ayubowan*, donkey," the jackal greeted him.

The donkey brayed.

"The lion is dying and he asked me to find some intelligent animal to be crowned as the king of the jungle before he passes away. He asked me to wear his crown but I said I would like to be free rather than being confined to the royal den. I suggested that you are the ideal animal to get that honour," the jackal told the dumbfounded donkey, who paused for a moment to digest the jackal's words. A jackal was not an animal to be trusted.

"The Lion King likes you because you don't eat meat and, therefore, you can win the trust of most animals. He also likes you because you are gentle and minds your own business. There are many contenders, but if you like to be the king you have got to hurry," the jackal said.

The donkey agreed and the jackal led him to the lion's den.

"Oh Lion King, I found the most intelligent animal in the jungle to be crowned as the new king," he said.

Donkey meat was not something the lion would have

relished under normal circumstances. It was hard times. He lunged at the donkey with a meek roar. The donkey was fleet-footed and escaped into the jungle.

"Couldn't you hold that donkey with your mighty paws which have even felled gigantic elephants. I will try to bring it once more," the jackal said running after the donkey.

He approached the donkey, now cowering behind a bush. "Why did you run away, you donkey? The king doesn't like to hand over his crown to a weak, foolish animal. He pounced at you to see how strong you are. Don't be afraid. He won't harm you. Show him that you are fearless," said the jackal.

The donkey, after hearing these assurances, went to the lion which lunged at him again. The donkey tried to ward off the attack, but the lion broke its neck with one wild swing of a paw.

The hungry lion began to eat the donkey.

"Chi, chi*, Sir. Is this how the king of the jungle must consume his royal meal? Don't forget your manners even in your old age. Shouldn't you wash and cleanse yourself before a meal? I have seen the Lion Queen going through her cleaning routine all the time. I live not very far from this den and have seen both of you having your meals in a dignified manner," said the jackal. Its mouth watered, looking at the bleeding donkey.

"Yes, that is true," said the lion as he left for a dip in the little stream that flowed at the edge of the forest.

The jackal couldn't resist the temptation to eat the donkey's brain. It was the tastiest part of any animal and people thought that the jackal was intelligent because it ate the brains of other animals.

The jackal broke the skull of the donkey, ate its brain greedily, went to the corner of the den and rested.

The lion came from the bath, water dripping from its

mane, sat down near the dead donkey and looked for the brain. The jackal watched the lion as if nothing had happened.

"Where is the brain, jackal? Did you eat it?" the lion roared.

"Why should I eat someone else's prey? I am still young and strong enough to hunt my own game. Do you think the donkey would have returned a second time to be killed by you if it had a brain?"

The lion agreed with the jackal, shaking his head in approval, and began eating other parts of the donkey.

Story III

The Monkeys And The Hat Seller

A hat seller was walking through a village to sell his produce. He had multi-coloured hats in an open box that rested on his head and he carried some in his hands.

He was singing, talking loudly and cracking jokes about the quality of his hats to attract customers. It was a hot, humid day and business was bad. He could only sell a few hats to some people working in the paddy fields, who promised to pay the next time he visited the village. He did not like to sell his hats on credit but had little choice. It helped lighten the load on his head and he could show his wife, who made the hats, that her products were selling well.

Village children ran towards him to look his box but he chased them away because they had dirty hands and could sully the hats.

It was now midday. The hat seller was hungry and tired. He sat under the shade of a tree, eased his box onto the ground and had his lunch, leaning against the tree.

Soon, he was feeling drowsy. He covered his face with a

hat to protect it from the rays of the sun filtering through the branches. He woke up suddenly to rustling sounds and found that the box was empty. He got up and walked around, looking in the bushes, wondering if children were playing pranks or somebody had stolen the hats.

He saw a villager passing by, going to the river to have a bath. The hat seller asked him whether he had met anyone on the road carrying a box. "I was just having a nap under this tree after a little lunch and when I woke up all my hats were gone," he told the villager. The man laughed and waved his hands, pointing to the trees.

A large number of monkeys were sitting on several branches, wearing his hats.

The seller gesticulated wildly trying to chase the monkeys thinking that they would throw the hats and go away. The primates also gesticulated wildly, imitating the hat seller. He picked up stones and threw at the monkeys. The animals plucked mangoes from the tree and threw them at him. He shouted and the monkeys snarled.

The villager was laughing, looking at the man and the monkeys. "What will you give me if I get your hats back?" the man asked.

"I will present you with the best hat of the lot. I don't have money to give you because business has been bad."

"Then, give me your hat," the villagers said.

The villager looked at the monkeys, wore the hat and raised it above his head. The monkeys did the same thing. Then he threw away his hat.

The monkeys too threw the hats away just as the man had done. The hat seller picked up all his hats and put them in the box. He thanked the villager profusely, presented him with two good hats and left, whistling a song and cursing the monkeys.

Story IV

The Jackal And His Crocodile Bride

The jackal and the crocodile were once good friends who became rivals because of a small incident.

One day, a jackal was waiting at a river bank, breathing deeply and his mouth watering as the wind brought with it the smell of a dead elephant on the other side of the river.

Elephant meat was a rarity on a jackal's menu and he was thinking of a way to cross the river when he saw a mud and weed-covered crocodile basking alone on a rock.

"*Ayubowan*, crocodile, all alone, no?" said the jackal greeting the croc. "Still haven't thought of marriage? How long can a handsome crocodile like you survive in this lonely waters without a wife to look after you? What will happen when you get older?"

The crocodile moved closer to the jackal.

"Look how handsome and strong you are. God, look at those beautiful teeth! I am surprised to see you without a wife at this age. Are you going to grow old and die a bachelor? Look at me. I have many wives and I cannot keep track of them," said the jackal, howling as if he was calling his concubines. "I can still get more wives."

"All the females in my clan are married and I am the only one left," said the crocodile shyly.

The smell of the rotting elephant was overpowering.

"Listen my friend. I know a beautiful crocodile in a lake beyond that forest. In fact, I am travelling there today to meet her parents to discuss some other matter. If you like, I can put in a word for you."

The crocodile was ecstatic.

"Please help me find a bride, dear jackal. I will do anything for you. I can even catch fish and tortoise for you. How will you get to the other side?"

"Yes, yes, fish and tortoise are always welcome. I am thinking of a way to cross the river. I could have hitched a ride on the canoe over there but today I don't see anyone using it. I cannot use an oar or a boat as humans do. I thought of swimming but I am not much of a swimmer, you know!" the jackal said.

"No problem. Jump on to my back and I will take you across."

So, the jackal jumped on to the back of the crocodile and safely landed on the other side of the river.

The jackal asked the crocodile to come in the evening to take him back. It ate elephant meat to its heart's content. After a long nap to digest his meal, the jackal went back to the river. His friend was waiting for him. He climbed on to the crocodile's back.

"I spoke to the father of the bride and he was very happy about the news but the mother and daughter have gone hunting. I will be able to speak to them only tomorrow."

The next day, the crocodile took the jackal to the other side of the river and again waited until sunset.

That day the jackal said he had met the prospective

bride and she was anxious to meet the crocodile to finalize wedding arrangements. The jackal rode on the back of the crocodile on seven mornings and seven evenings, until only the skeleton of the elephant remained. On the last day the crocodile waited for the jackal as usual.

"Everything has been finalized, dear crocodile. Tomorrow night the bride will wait on the other side of the river. You have to go there at midnight and bring your beautiful bride to your river," said the jackal while crossing.

The jackal landed safely on the other side and took a few steps away from striking distance of the crocodile.

"Hey croc! I have never seen a foolish animal like you. Who will give a bride to a fat, ugly cannibal like you! There are no crocodiles on the other side. All I wanted to do was to eat that fat elephant rotting on the other side. Anyway, thank you for the rides," the jackal shouted, howling.

The furious crocodile rushed to the riverbank with its mouth wide open and lunged at the jackal who took to his heels. The crocodile-jackal rivalry, it is said in Sri Lanka, began on that day.

Story V

The Flying Turtle

Rivers were running dry and even water in ponds were evaporating rapidly as a prolonged drought held a viselike grip on a fertile, forested area.

In a small pond, under the shade of withering trees, a turtle lived a solitary life. It survived by eating dead fish and as the water became scarcer, the turtle knew its days were numbered.

A hungry jackal was in the habit of coming to the pond looking for an opportunity to devour the turtle. One night, when the turtle was on one of its nocturnal wanderings looking for an escape route to another pond, it stumbled upon the jackal.

The turtle withdrew into its shell. The fox did not want this close encounter to be in vain and tried all the tricks to coax its prey to surrender. All its efforts were fruitless.

The next day, the turtle saw two storks looking to hunt fish with their long beaks. "All the fish in this pond are dead and the same thing will happen to you if this cursed drought goes on for some more days," the turtle told the birds.

"We are on our way to a pond with lot of fish in the next jungle and we landed after seeing you here, wondering what you are still doing in this heap of mud," said a stork.

"Ané* Sirs, can you please take me to a pond with lot of water? I will help you to catch more fish. There is a jackal trying to eat me and there are also wild elephants roaming about in the night and I fear being trampled by them."

The storks thought for a moment. "But how can we take you? You can't fly."

The turtle suggested a plan. "Can you please find a stick? You both can hold the ends of the stick in your beaks and fly and I will bite hard onto the stick until you land safely."

The storks liked the idea but warned that the turtle should never open its mouth while in the air.

So the turtle bit hard on the stick. The birds took both its ends into their beaks and began to fly.

The fox, sleeping near a parched field, woke up in time to see the wonder of the flying turtle. He rubbed his eyes. "Am I going mad or am I seeing a flying turtle?" asked the jackal as it began to chase the shadow of the flying trio.

The turtle was overjoyed at outwitting the jackal, and felt he must express himself. He opened its mouth to abuse the jackal, fell to the ground crushing its shell and became easy meat for the famished jackal.

Story VI

The Cobra, The Viper And The Mongoose

One bright summer day, a mother left her child in a clay tub of water and left the house to run an errand.

The baby was playing with a coconut shell, filling it with water and pouring it over his head and sloshing the water with his tiny hands.

A thirsty cobra happened to slither past the house and saw the child playing with water. Cobras are treated with respect in rural Sri Lanka, as the reptiles seldom inflict harm on human beings unless provoked.

Legend has it that one day a blind man trampled a cobra and the reptile turned to attack the man but spared him as he was blind.

In our story, the cobra crept inside the child's tub and drank water. The baby touched the cobra and even hit it with the coconut shell. The reptile, however, ignored the child, knowing it was all done in play.

The cobra quenched its thirst and slithered slowly out of the tub and left the home. While on its way to an anthill to rest, it came across a viper looking for water. Seeing the drops of water on the cobra's mouth the viper wanted to know where it could get a drink. The cobra did not reveal the source as it knew the viper was vicious when it came into contact with human beings.

"Hey viper, I cannot tell you where I found the water because you are not a creature of cultured habits and patience," the cobra said.

The viper, which was almost dying of thirst, pleaded with the cobra to guide it to the source of water and promised that it would not harm anybody.

The cobra relented.

The viper crept towards the house and found the tub.

It stretched its body languidly and began to drink the water. The playful child hit the viper with his hands and the coconut shell. When the child hit its head again, the viper lost its temper and flashed its venomous fangs.

The cobra, which was resting in its anthill abode, had a premonition that the viper would not keep its word, and it began to slither towards the house. On the way, it met the viper with blood on its mouth.

"Did you kill the child?" the cobra asked the viper but the latter ignored the question and tried to escape into the thick undergrowth of the jungle.

The infuriated cobra grabbed the viper by its neck and swallowed it.

It then rushed to the home and found the child lying motionless in the tub. The cobra kept its mouth at the wound and sucked the viper's venom out of the child's body.

The child opened his eyes and started playing with the coconut shell and hitting the head of the cobra.

A thirsty mongoose, on the trail of water, arrived at the home, and saw the cobra curled up on the child's leg and thought it was trying to bite the infant. It pounced on the cobra and killed it after a ferocious fight in the tub and later on the ground.

When the child's mother returned, she saw the mongoose with blood on its mouth and thought it had killed her child. She picked up a stick and beat the mongoose to death.

Even today, if a cobra meets a viper, their fight unto death ends with the cobra swallowing the viper. If a cobra and a mongoose happen to meet, the encounter will be deadly, ending with the mongoose killing the cobra.

The mongoose is said to chew upon the leaves of a plant to recover from a cobra attack. Native physicians in Sri Lanka, who tend to people bitten by poisonous snakes, even today use these leaves to make concoctions to counter venom.

Story VII

The Injured Horse

A man was riding a horse for several days and the beast developed a severe rash on its back, which was soon infected. The infection spread to other parts of the body, forcing him to abandon the animal.

An oil trader, who was passing by, took pity on the horse which was writhing on the ground. He applied some medicinal oils on the infected areas and went on his way.

A rag dealer, who was taking a heap of old clothes for sale in a nearby town, saw the suffering horse, covered its wounds with rags, poured more oil onto the bandages and went on his way.

A farmer, who was preparing a plot of land for cultivation by the side of the forest path, was setting dry bushes on fire. Sparks from the blazing fire landed on the horse, engulfing the injured animal's bandages.

The horse got up with difficulty and began to run hither and thither and entered a *pengiri* (citronella) cultivation. The plants immediately caught fire and in a few minutes the entire plantation was destroyed.

The owner of the plantation went to the king with his

complaint. "My Lord, a horse with rotting skin, covered in burning oil rags, ran into my plantation and destroyed it. Please find the owner of this horse, punish him and ask him to pay me damages."

The king thought for a while.

"It is not the fault of the man who applied oil to the beast's wounds and bandaged them," said the king.

"He did it with the good intention of saving the life of the stricken animal. It is neither the fault of man who owned the horse that died in the fire nor the farmer who set fire to dry bushes to clear the forest. It is your own fault for not securing the fence surrounding the property".

Story VIII

How The Hare And The Fox Ate Milk Rice

A hare and a fox were once sweeping a garden when they found two pumpkin seeds. They dug two holes in the ground and planted them, promising to look after a sapling each.

The fox, always lazy, urinated on his creeper while the hare drew water from the well and poured it on its plant. The pumpkin creeper of the fox withered and died. The hare, always kind to its friend, promised to share his pumpkin when it matured.

The pumpkin was, however, not enough to satiate the fox's hunger and it thought of ways to get more food with the help of the hare.

There was a road meandering through the forest which was used by farmers to take their produce to a village fair. The fox asked the hare to lie on the road pretending to be dead and when the farmers were passing by, the fox cried out: "Hey you farmers, keep your bags down and take this dead hare away."

When the farmers, who had heard stories about the efficacy of hare stew for their health, kept their loads down to pick up the hare it ran away and the fox stole their rice bags and scampered into the jungle.

Back in the cave, the fox began to cook pumpkin milk rice and asked the hare to fetch stalkless *kenda** leaves to wrap the balls of rice. This was a ruse employed by the cunning fox to eat the whole pot of milk rice.

Unable to find stalkless *kenda* leaves, the hare returned after a long time and ate the little rice left in the pot. The fox was asleep on the ground after the heavy meal, plugging his backside with coconut husk to block its overfilled stomach.

The fox became sick and asked the hare to remove the coconut husk from its back.

When the hare pulled out the plug, excrement splattered on its body. It ran to a meadow and rolled several times over the dewy grass and came home quite clean.

The fox wanted to know how the hare had returned to the den, squeaky clean.

The hare explained that it was the washer woman who was beating clothes on a stone near the river, who cleaned him with soap and water.

The fox trotted off to the riverside and asked the washer woman to clean it as well.

The washerwoman grabbed the fox's hind legs and thrashed it on the stone, shouting, "You are the fox that ate all my chickens." Thud!

"I will clean you... clean the life out of you."
Thud! Thud!

Story IX

Magic Of The Magpie

A magpie (*polkichcha**) laid two eggs in a nest but when the wind blew hard they fell into an '*eraminia**' bush of thorns. The bird tried to retrieve the eggs but it could not do so because of the sharp, tangled nature of the thorns. The bird asked a farmer to clear the thorns with his machete but he refused.

The magpie befriended a porcupine and asked it to destroy the farmer's paddy crop.

When the porcupine refused, the bird asked a hunter to kill the porcupine. When the hunter said 'no', as he was not fond of porcupine meat, the magpie befriended an elephant by picking out blood-sucking flies from its back and pleaded with it to kill the hunter. The jumbo refused because the hunter had a gun.

The magpie asked the *heeraluwa** lizard to creep up the elephant's trunk, but it said 'no'.

The bird then asked a hawk to kill the *heeraluwa*. The only creature that instilled mortal fear in elephants was the tiny *heeraluwa* lizard which could creep through its trunk and create havoc. The hawk refused to kill the *heeraluwa*.

The magpie lamented, perched on a branch: "The hawk won't kill the *heeraluwa*, which won't creep up the elephant's trunk. The elephant won't kill the hunter who refuses to kill the porcupine. The porcupine won't destroy the crop of the farmer who refuses to help me retrieve my eggs by cutting thorns with his machete."

A fox was passing by and wanted to know the reason behind the bird's sorrow. The magpie explained the problem.

The fox promised to help and began to snarl at the hawk, the hawk began to peck at the *heeraluwa* lizard, the *heeraluwa* began creeping up the elephant's trunk, the elephant began to gore the hunter, the hunter began to shoot the porcupine, the porcupine began to eat the farmer's paddy crop, the farmer began to cut the thorns with his machete and the magpie retrieved her two eggs.

Story X

The Trapped Deer And A Sly Jackal

A severe drought had dried up every water hole in the jungle and the animals were wandering around looking for a water source to quench their thirst.

Among the animals was a deer. A crow was cawing on a tree and the deer spoke to him.

"Hello crow, you seem to be happy and content. Look at me. There's not a drop of water to drink in our jungle and I am dying of thirst."

The crow replied: "I know a place where there is lot of water, but that is in another jungle and about half day's walk for you from here. I can take you there."

The deer thanked the crow and followed him.

On the way, they met a jackal panting, with its tongue hanging loosely.

"Oh deer, tell me where I can find a drop of water. I am dying of thirst."

"Come with us, jackal. We are going to a place where there is a lot of water," said the deer sprinting to catch up with the crow that was flying low overhead. The jackal started to follow the deer, its mouth watering at the sight of the deer's stomach. The jackal hadn't eaten venison for a long time.

So, the three of them reached a pond full of water and drank to their heart's content. The trio decided to go looking for food and a place to rest for the night.

A *veddha** (an aborigine who lived in the jungle and hunted animals for food) was passing by and came to the pond to drink water. He noticed the hoof prints of a deer and decided to set a trap.

"Today is my lucky day," the *veddha* thought. "It looks like a full grown deer and one which can provide meat for me and my family for weeks. What's better than dried venison and bee's honey!" His mouth watered at the thought.

He followed the hoof prints that disappeared into a grove of trees. He was now close enough to smell the deer.

The next day, the *veddha* came near the pond and hid behind a tree and saw the deer, jackal and the crow drinking water.

When night fell, he set a trap made up of deer hide and went home.

The jackal noticed the footprints of the man near the pond and knew that the deer's days were numbered. It decided to stay by the side of the deer and asked it to remain near the pond for some more days. "What is the use of going to the jungle where we came from? There is not a cloud in the sky and there is no sign of rain. Let us stay here until the rains come," said the jackal, smacking its lips.

The deer and crow agreed. The next morning, while the trio was going to the pond to drink water, the deer was caught in the trap.

It struggled hard to set itself free but the knots tightened around its neck.

The crow tried to peck at the trap to free its friend from certain death but its efforts were in vain. The deer cried in pain.

The jackal cowered behind a bush salivating, thinking about the deer's tasty, juicy belly that was going to be his dinner. Human beings had no taste for its belly and so it ended up being easy pickings for jackals.

The crow flew to the place where the jackal was hiding and pleaded with it to save the deer. "Jackal, you have sharp teeth. Please help our friend to escape. Don't you remember we became friends many days ago when we were searching for water? Wasn't it I who helped you to find water to save your life? Please bite hard and loosen the trap."

With droopy eyes and a tongue lolling to one side of its mouth, the jackal sported a sad face. "Don't you know how sad I am? What can I do, dear crow? A few days ago I was biting into an elephant skull and damaged my teeth. I can hardly bite my food now with all these shaky teeth," said the jackal. "I am very sad, but the *veddha* will be soon here with his axe," it sighed.

The crow flew away, landed near the deer, and tried once more to free the animal.

The deer said it was thirsty. So, the crow brought water from the pond in its beak and poured into the deer's mouth.

"The jackal is not willing to help you. He says his teeth are damaged. If the *veddha* comes here with his axe he will surely kill you. You must pretend as if you are dead, when he approaches you. I will come and poke at your eyes and he will think you are dead. As he unties the straps get up and run as far as your legs can carry you. I will follow you," said the crow.

The deer agreed.

The *veddha* came in the evening and the crow cried out loudly, warning the deer of the approaching hunter. The deer acted as if it was dead. As the *veddha* approached the deer, the crow landed on its body and pretended to poke at the eyes.

The jackal got up, stretched and straightened its body, still hiding behind the bush.

The *veddha* was sure the deer was dead, shooed away the crow and loosened the trap.

The deer got up and sprinted into the bushes as fast it could. The stunned *veddha* did not understand what was happening. He picked up his axe and threw it at the deer. The axe missed its target and hit the jackal, killing it instantly. The crow let out victorious cries as it flew into the woods in search of its friend.

Story XI

A Foolish Bird And 'Mee' Flowers

A bird hatched three eggs on a rock. When the chicks grew a little bigger she flew away every morning looking for food to feed them.

Every afternoon and evening, she brought small insects and fruits for them.

One day she brought a beakful of '*mee*'* flowers. The flowers looked like small berries and had a soft pale skin hiding sweet sap. Birds were fond of these flowers, and villagers also picked them early in the morning before the birds and other rodents reached them.

(Even today, the raw 'Mee' flower is a principal ingredient in a steamed sweet called 'Helapa', which comes wrapped in 'Kenda' leaves. These flowers impart a flavour akin to dried grapes.)

The bird kept the flowers on the rock to eat them later. The next morning, when she flew away to find more food, she advised the chicks to look after the '*mee*' flowers as other birds and insects would try to steal them.

The chicks assured their mother that they would remain alert and aware of their surroundings.

The rock became very hot during the day and the flowers shrank as its sap dried in the sun and disappeared.

The mother bird came back in the evening with food for her little ones.

"Did you all eat my flowers?" she asked when she couldn't see any of the 'mee' flowers. "Didn't I ask you to look after them?"

The little birds did not know what happened to the flowers and said they did not eat them. The mother bird did not believe them.

"How can you lie to me? When I left in the morning, the flowers were here and didn't I ask you to look after them? What could have happened? You three must have eaten them. I was concerned because the sweetness of these flowers will give you tummy aches."

"Yes, they were there when you left but we did not see them after that," the chicks said.

Enraged, she began pecking ferociously at them. The chicks died.

The throne of *Sakhra Deva** (King of the Gods) began to heat up. When anything bad happened to good creatures on earth, his seat began to warm, calling for his immediate attention to the problem. He looked down and saw what the foolish bird had done to her innocent chicks.

Sakhra Deva called for rain. The 'mee' flowers, which were still on the rock, absorbed water and began expanding. The bird realized what a terrible thing she had done to her chicks and started weeping. She cried for days, did not go out looking for food and starved herself to death.

Story XII

The Lion And The Bull

A lion was friendly with a bull and it was seen by all the animals in the jungle as a strange relationship.

The beasts were traditional enemies, fearful of each other's power. Often, bulls became victims of lions, but not without a prolonged fight. While the lions were excellent hunters, they often suffered fatal injuries because of the curved horns of the bulls. The bulls could also toss the lions high up in the air and trample them to death.

There was a lazy jackal in the jungle, which hung around the lion's den to eat carrion. The jackal, which had a voracious appetite, was jealous of the friendship between the lion and the bull and plotted to create a rift between them.

One fine summer morning, the jackal appeared before the lion and inquired about his wellbeing.

"Sire, you are the king of jungle and the jackal clan conveys their well wishes to you," said the jackal standing a few feet away from the lion as a mark of respect. "However, My Lord, of late we have been worried about your strange friendship with that uncouth bull. The foolish bull is not an animal worthy of your royal attention. Your ancestors would have never allowed such a lowly beast into your den. Recently, he told me that he was not scared of your strength and said soon he would oust you from the throne and capture power."

The lion thought for a moment. He had no respect for the jackal but he was one of the channels the lion trusted to get gossip about happenings in the jungle.

The lion said he did not believe what the jackal said about the bull. "The bull has proved to be a very faithful friend. He has never shown any interest in becoming a leader of the animals." The lion chased the jackal away.

The jackal went to meet the bull, which was happily grazing in a meadow. "Good morning, dear friend," the jackal addressed the bull and sprawled on the grass. "You know I am a good friend of yours. I was enraged by what the lion said about you the other day."

"What did he say?" asked the bull shifting cud from one side of his jaw to the other, eyeing the jackal suspiciously.

"He said you are the most foolish animal in the jungle and he was not scared of your horns. He said he could kill you with one roar."

The bull was hurt. "He should not tell things like that when we remain the best of friends."

The bull went to the lion's den. "Why do you talk ill of me to other animals? Am I not your best friend in the jungle? Your big paws and your roar cannot kill me."

The bull snorted, thumped his hooves on the ground and challenged the lion to a fight. The lion roared with all his might and the bull jumped and gored his friend.

The lion's roar split the bull's eardrums killing it instantly while the lion succumbed to his injuries.

The jackal, who had been yearning to taste lion meat, summoned its kith and kin and they enjoyed a sumptuous feast of the meat from two animals for several days.

Story XIII

The Farmer And The Cattle-Stealing Leopard

A leopard was in the habit of attacking and eating cattle belonging to a farmer, on the outskirts of a jungle. The farmer built a strong fence with solid timber around the animal pen, but the leopard did not stop its nightly raids.

One day, the farmer decided to set a trap to catch the leopard. He dug a deep pit near the area where he found leopard tracks and covered it with dry leaves. The next morning, when he went to check the trap, he saw the leopard had fallen into the pit. It looked very weak and sad.

"Please let me out, Sir. I will never steal your cattle again. I have been starving the whole night and I am very hungry," the leopard wept.

The farmer felt sorry and kept a ladder for the beast to climb out of the pit. Soon, the animal was out of the pit and it lunged towards the man to eat him.

"Why are you trying to eat me? Am I not the one who set you free from the trap?" he asked.

"I am hungry. I have been starving the whole night. Do

you want me to die of hunger?" the leopard asked, licking its lips.

"This is not fair. It is true that I set a trap to stop you killing my cattle. But I freed you from certain death. We will go and ask some one to see whether you have any moral right to eat me."

The leopard agreed.

First, they approached a mango tree. The leopard asked: "Mango tree, this man set a trap to catch me and I went hungry the whole night. Do I have the right to eat him?"

The mango tree replied: "Don't let this man escape. He is more wicked than an animal. He eats my fruits, boils my leaves and roots and drinks that liquid to stay healthy. He kills and eats the birds that sleep and make nests in my tree. He cuts my branches to make furniture. Very soon, he will cut me down and make a house. Eat this man,"

The farmer said, "We will meet someone else and ask for another opinion."

They then approached a goat.

"Oh goat! Listen to me. I saved this leopard from a trap I had made to catch it for eating my cattle. Now he is trying to eat me. Does he have the right to do so?" the farmer asked.

"Eat the man, dear leopard. He is a cruel creature. He steals my kids and sell them to the butcher. He drinks the milk I save for the kids, eats the meat of my relatives and when I become old he will sell me also to the butcher."

They noticed a jackal which was watching from a distance. "Oh jackal. We have heard of your great wisdom and we have come to you to consult about an important matter," said the man.

The jackal eyed man and leopard with suspicion, but decided to stay calm. He, of course, had a score to settle with the leopard. "Tell us the truth, dear jackal. I set a trap to catch this leopard because he was stealing my cattle. This morning I saw him inside the pit. I freed him because I felt sorry for him. Now, he wants to eat me as he is hungry."

The jackal thought for a moment.

"It is very difficult to arrive at a solution of this complicated problem. I would like to see a reenactment of the incident to arrive at a just decision," he said.

So the three of them went near the trap. The leopard jumped into the pit and the farmer covered it with dry leaves.

"You idiot farmer, cover the pit with earth and sand, stone and thorns and never let this beast escape if you want to save your life and your cattle," said the jackal.

The farmer buried the leopard alive, ignoring his roars for mercy and gifted the jackal with a fat, fully-grown fowl as a present.

Story XIV

How The Jackal Got Rid Of Its Ticks

A jackal was infested with ticks. It did everything to get rid of the annoying insects which did not allow it to sleep well and prevented it from hunting for food.

The jackal tried rolling in the sand and grass, rubbing its body for hours, went through thickets brushing against the underbrush and scratching every area of its body where the paws reached. The ticks still flourished.

Animals chased it away from their territories and, worst of all, its own kith and kin started keeping a distance from it for fear of being infested.

The jackal became weak, as it could not hunt anymore. The overpowering stench of its festering wounds alerted its prey well in advance.

One day, the jackal went to a river and was lying down on the grass looking at otters gnawing down trees to make a nest.

The otters were suspicious of the jackal as it had hunted their little ones on a number of occasions but one old otter noticed its helplessness and spoke to the animal.

"Hey jackal, is anything the matter? You are half the size of your usual self. Are you unwell?" asked the otter, flashing a toothy smile.

"I am fed up with life, dear otter. Look at me. I am infested with ticks. I tried many treatments but they won't go away. Other animals and my own relatives have started avoiding me," said the jackal, turning over and rubbing its back on the wet grass.

The otter family was looking at the jackal. They were sad about its plight though it was not an animal to be trusted.

"Hey otter! Don't you have ticks?" asked the jackal looking at the bushy coat of the otter. "You have such long hair."

The otter laughed. "Can ticks live in water like us?"

The jackal stood up. "I now know what to do. Thank you, otter," said the animal as it ran away to sneak into a farmer's garden.

Nocturnal raids by jackals on his chicken pen had become a major problem for the farmer and he set traps every night to catch the intruders.

The jackal tiptoed carefully across the farm to pick up a piece of coconut husk and ran to the river. As its legs started getting wet the jackal felt the ticks trying to avoid the water and climb higher, clinging to its body. The jackal went further until only its head was above water. All the ticks scrambled to reach its head to avoid drowning. The jackal immersed his head in the water, holding the coconut husk above him. The ticks jumped onto the coconut husk thinking that it was the jackal's tail.

It slowly released the coconut husk and ran to the river bank. The husk floated away with all the ticks, like a boat carrying passengers. The jackal howled triumphantly, thanked the otters and ran free into the jungle.

Story XV

When The Fox Invited The Stork To Dinner

One day a fox invited a stork to come for a meal. Though it was a strange relationship, they both liked each other's company.

Sometimes the stork threw a fish or two at the fox if it was too full to eat anymore.

One day, when the stork went to the fox's den, dinner was served on two flat plates. All the plates at its house were like that. The fox consumed all what was on the plate but the stork pushed away the food after many unsuccessful attempts to manoeuvre its long beak.

When the stork courteously refused the food, the fox ate that too. The stork went home hungry.

A few days later, it was stork's turn to repay the fox's kindness and invited it for dinner. The fox readily agreed and went along with its friend. It's mouth watered as it smelled cooked fish.

The bird served fish in two jugs with long necks. While the stork relished the food, the fox could not eat because its face got stuck in the narrow mouth of the jug. He watched hungrily as the stork ate his dinner with relish using his long beak like a pair of giant chopsticks.

When the stork asked why the fox did not want to eat, it whined that it had an allergy to cooked fish. The stork finished fox's plate too. They remained friends after these incidents, but never invited each other for a meal again.

Story XVI

The Quails And The 'Veddhas'

The *veddhas* are original inhabitants of Sri Lanka, driven into the forests by invaders. They survived down the ages by hunting for food and one of their delicacies was quail.

Quail meat had a delectable flavour and the birds were well-fed and plump when they flew into the island during the warm season. The birds were smart and agile and could dodge the *veddhas'* arrows and spears with ease. The *veddhas* then weaved nets from fibers they gathered in the wild and threw them over the birds when they rested on the ground. The quails were alarmed at the rate at which their kind was being hunted and their leaders devised a plan to defeat the hunters.

One day, the birds were feeding on the ground and a group of *veddhas* threw a net over them. "United We Survive," shouted a leader and all the birds flapped their wings together, soaring and flying away with the net. It is said that they taught the trick to other birds, forcing the *veddhas* to look for alternate sources of food to survive.

PART VII

Other Rural Stories

In the early part of the book, we covered the towering figures inhabiting Sri Lankan folktales, like Andare and Maha Dena Muththa. The tales in the following pages are of simple people living in small agricultural settlements and the tragicomic stories that revolve around their simple lives.

Humans in these settings also have strong thematic connections with animals and inanimate objects, creating delightful twists in the tales.

Story I

A Mother's Milk Is Never Measured

There was once a woman in a small village who had fallen on hard times after her husband died. She was finding it difficult to get even the basic necessities of life.

In despair, she decided one day to visit her married son who lived in another village.

She trudged to the river bank where she collected some reeds to weave a bag. "This should be enough," she said to herself. "I can get rice from my son to fill this bag."

When she reached the house, the daughter-in-law welcomed her with some trepidation. They had not maintained contact with the woman. They were now people of status in society and kept aloof from poorer folk.

The old woman sat on the floor and inquired whether her son was at home.

The woman went inside. After what seemed almost an hour, the son came and sat on the floor. He did not ask about her health or her way of living or about the house where he was born or about his childhood friends.

"My son, I have not eaten for days after your father died. I am old and can't work the fields. There is also a drought in our village. Can you give me some rice?"

The son called out to his wife and asked her to give a '*hundu*'* of rice to his mother. The wife filled one half of a coconut shell and poured it into the old woman's reed bag.

The mother looked at the vast expanse of just-harvested rice paddies around the house and the huge quantity of paddy drying on mats in the compound.

"My son, did I measure milk when I fed you from my breasts?" the old woman asked. The son just looked at her, shook his head and went inside without saying a word.

She placed the bag on the ground and stepped out of the house.

Story II

How We Got Sweet Potatoes

Deep in the heart of Sri Lanka, in a small village, there lived a poor widow who had a beautiful daughter. All the young men in the village were besotted with her angelic charm and wanted to marry her. The mother, however, wanted her to wed a rich man.

The woman, knowing that dowry would play an important role in a marriage, worked hard in other people's homes and rice fields to save money.

After a long search and through the services of a marriage broker, the mother found a wealthy man who lived in the city. Smitten by the girl's beauty, the man married her, although the dowry was a paltry one.

The seasons dawned and waned. The mother grew old and fell on hard times. She began begging in the streets and knocking at the doors of her neighbours, asking for food.

One day, she went to visit her daughter who lived in a very large house surrounded by rice paddies and a farm with lot of cows and horses. The old woman was very happy that her daughter now led a comfortable life. She entered the house and called out to her daughter who was busy in the kitchen cooking lunch.

The daughter could not recognize her emaciated mother, clothed in rags. "I thought you were dead," said the woman peering outside to see whether any of her husband's relatives were watching them.

The old woman's mouth watered as the scent of flavoured rice wafted out from the kitchen. "My daughter, I have been starving for many days. Please give me some rice to quell my hunger," she pleaded.

The daughter was embarrassed by her mother's shabby appearance and chased her away, saying she had no rice to give her. The old woman went away crying.

The woman went to the kitchen to check the pot on the stove and found that the rice had turned into blood. She threw away the contents. Legend says it was *Sakhra Deva*, the King of Gods, who turned the rice in the pot into blood after hearing the old woman's cries.

After the husband returned home for lunch, he found that his wife had thrown away the pot of rice. He was furious and rained blows on his wife and threw her out of the house. As further punishment, the King of Gods also reduced the daughter to beggary, who began wandering in the streets, pleading for food like her mother did.

After a few days, Sakhra Deva felt compassionate and appeared before the mother and daughter and asked them to dig up the place where the daughter had emptied the pot of rice. After digging a few inches of the earth, they found a root which Sri Lankans today call the '*batale*' yam.

Batale is the Sinhala name for the tuberous root vegetable called sweet potato. '*Bata*' means cooked rice in Sinhala and '*le*' is blood. From that day on, blood-coloured sweet potatoes became a staple food for the poor.

Story III

Seven Mendicants And A Pot of Rice Porridge

Seven mendicants once met in an *'ambalama'*.

The men planned to make some rice porridge. They usually carried cloth satchels slung over their shoulders to collect alms, usually rice and other types of food, because the poor villagers were unable to give cash as donations.

One man collected firewood while another borrowed a pot from a nearby house and another brought water from a *'pinthaliya'**.

A mendicant made a hearth with three stones, lighted a fire and asked the others to put in their contribution to the pot of porridge, which was going to be their dinner.

"This is a good idea. Here is my contribution," said the oldest of the seven, putting his hand into his satchel and adding his share of rice into the pot, using a closed fist, and asking others to follow his example. Everyone did the same.

One of the mendicants stirred the pot with a stick until it boiled over. It was now time to drink the porridge.

Another mendicant took a coconut ladle, stirred the

boiling pot and emptied a spoonful into the bowl of the senior among them. The ladle had nothing but hot water.

Everyone rested chins on their hands and looked blankly at the pot, at each other and then sat staring silently at the ground.

What really happened was that each mendicant was trying to capitalize on the generosity of the other by acting as if they were putting their share of rice into the pot. They did not open their closed fists.

The popular Sri Lankan proverb, *"Like seven mendicants' pot of porridge"*, to describe a project gone astray due to insufficient or sham contributions from the people involved, comes from this tale.

Story IV

The Flying Cotton Ball And A Greedy Cousin

Two sisters once lived in a village in the deep interior of the island. Each one had a daughter.

One fine day, one of the daughters was whirling cotton on a spinning wheel while her mother was helping by rolling the cotton into balls. All of a sudden, a ball of cotton flew away with the wind. The mother reprimanded the daughter for being so careless and asked her to bring it back.

The girl ran after the ball of cotton as it flew away, spinning and rolling and circling over the trees. She came across a lame farmer watering his betel leaf cultivation.

The man asked the girl to help him draw water from the well. "My leg does not allow me to do heavy work. However, who will feed me if I don't work?"

The girl felt sorry for him and drew water from the well which the farmer splashed over his plants. The lame man thanked her saying, "When you come again this away, I will give you good betel leaves to take home."

She continued to run after the cotton ball when she saw a dog tied to a tree. "Sister, please tie me to a tree where there is shade. Here, the sun is burning me. I will give you some venison to take home when you are passing through here the next time," the dog said.

She looked up and saw the tree had no leaves and the dog was exposed to the blazing son. So she tied the animal to a leafy tree with a cool canopy.

Again, she chased the cotton ball, which got entangled in a cane bush. She was trying to remove the ball with a long stick when a king happened to pass by, riding a richly caparisoned elephant.

"What are you doing out in this hot sun?" the king asked her.

"I am trying to retrieve the cotton ball from the cane bush. When we were spinning cotton, this ball flew away on a gust of wind and my mother asked me to catch it and bring it back," she said.

"I will help you to get it. Now, go to my palace and help cook a meal for me. I have thousands of soldiers but they only know how to fight wars. Nobody knows how to cook," the king said and took down the cotton ball.

The girl went to the palace and cooked a fine meal. The king had never eaten such tasty dishes and decided to give a present to the girl. He took her to his chamber which had many boxes of various sizes arranged against the walls. He asked her to take any box she liked. She selected the smallest box that was made of sandalwood.

"The contents in this box will enable you and your family to have a better future," said the king.

On her way home, she saw the dog tied to the shady tree. It gave her a thigh of a freshly hunted deer and told her to cook a good meal for her family.

She continued on her journey, passing the lame farmer's betel leaf garden. He thanked her again for helping him and gave her a bunch of betel leaves to take home.

The girl reached home carrying all the gifts: a box from the king, venison and betel leaves.

The family was astonished when the girl opened the sandalwood box. It was full of gems, gold coins and pearls.

The next day, her aunt started spinning cotton and threw a ball of cotton into the wind. She called her daughter, smacked her head and asked her to bring it back. The girl started to cry and ran after the cotton ball.

When she was passing the lame man's betel leaf plantation, the farmer asked for her help to draw water for the plants. She refused. "I have to catch the cotton ball."

When she passed the dog, the animal asked her to tie it to a tree with shade and promised to give her a good cut of venison if she helped him. The girl refused and continued to run after the ball.

Finally, the cotton ball got entangled in the cane bush. She was trying to remove it with a stick when the king came riding by on his elephant. He said: "I will release the cotton ball from the cane bush. Go to my palace and cook me a good meal."

The girl went to the palace kitchen and cooked lunch. However, the king did not eat the meal as it had no flavour, no colour and no aroma.

He took her to the chamber where there were many boxes and asked her to select one. She thought to herself: "My cousin was a fool to choose a small box. I will select the biggest one here and I am sure there will be more gems, gold coins and pearls than what was in her box."

"You have taken a box that you like. You must open this only in the presence of your parents," said the king before she left the palace.

The girl reached home and told the story to her parents.

In the evening, the family asked all the villagers to come and witness the wealth that her daughter had brought from the palace.

As the girl opened the box, cobras, vipers and various kinds of poisonous snakes sprang out of the box and began to sting the girl, her parents and everyone in the village. Even today, that village is known as *Palu Gama*, which means "village with no inhabitants."

Story V

The Golden Pumpkin

A hard-working cultivator one day found a pumpkin made of gold in his farm, while digging for some root vegetables under a banyan tree. He surmised that the pumpkin was a gift from *Sakhara Deva,* for the many good deeds he had performed over the years.

There were many thieves in the village so he gave the pumpkin to one of his close friends who lived in the town for safekeeping.

The farmer inquired about it every time he met his friend and the man assured that it was safe in his house.

One day, the farmer went to his friend and asked for his pumpkin. "I need some money and must sell it to a jeweller in the city."

His friend gave him a shiny, brass pumpkin.

The farmer took it away but on the way home he knew from the texture and the weight of the pumpkin that his friend had cheated him.

A few weeks after the incident, the farmer's friend and his wife wanted to go away on a pilgrimage and asked if the farmer could look after his son till they returned.

The farmer readily agreed.

When the friend and his wife returned after several days, they came to the farmer's house to take their son home. The farmer gave them a monkey.

The friend complained to the king about the incident. The farmer and the man were summoned to the royal court. The king listened patiently to both parties and pondered how a golden pumpkin had turned into a brass one and how a child became a monkey.

He then delivered the judgement, ordering the farmer to retun the man's son and asked the friend to return the golden pumpkin.

Story VI

The Salt Seller And The Crafty Donkey

A salt seller in a village had a donkey. He took his produce for sale in the town fair, placing the load on the donkey's back. He had to pass a shallow river on the way.

One day the donkey accidentally slipped on a mossy stone and fell into the water. The man helped the animal to its feet and pulled it to the banks. By then, the salt had dissolved in the water and the animal felt lighter. The donkey made it a habit to fall into the river every time it crossed the waterway on the way to the fair.

The man who thought that donkeys were foolish animals was surprised by its antics and decided to counter-attack.

The following week, the salt seller loaded the sack onto the animal's back and headed to the fair. The load felt lighter and the beast thought it was strange but continued walking happily.

When the donkey came to the stream it fell into the water as usual, thinking that would make the load lighter. But the unexpected happened. When it got out of water its load felt heavier than usual.

What the donkey did not know was that the man had loaded cotton onto its back. It lugged the load of wet cotton to the fair. Though there was nobody to buy wet cotton the man was happy that he had taught the donkey a lesson. The animal never fell into the water again.

Story VII

How Man Ended His Friendship With Elephants

When man began cultivating lands, encroaching the habitats of a wild elephant, the pachyderm began to strike back, destroying his crops and attacking the farmers.

It did not stop there. The jumbo harassed small animals, pulled down trees with bird nests, trampled the homes of smaller animals and drank whatever little water was left after droughts. Man and animals thought the elephant was crossing the limits of legitimate behaviour.

A man befriended a fox and planned to get rid of the rogue without understanding the elephant's behaviour. One day, the fox went to meet the elephant and said the animals in the jungle wanted to crown it as their king as there was no other creature to match its size and strength.

The fox said that all animals were waiting for the crowning ceremony and led the elephant through a marshy land. The fox crossed the land easily due to its lighter weight but when the elephant reached the middle of the swamp it began to slide into the mud.

The pachyderm cried for help as it began to submerge. It sank little by little up to the neck and began trumpeting.

The fox turned back and said that no one was going to help it. "This is the punishment you get for your cruelty. You have destroyed man's cultivations and broken our homes and left us thirsty during the drought by drinking all the water in the ponds."

The elephant asked whether the man had done the right thing by destroying its natural home by slashing and burning the jungle to cultivate the lands. Those things mattered little to the animals as they were preoccupied with finding a solution to their hunger and thirst, the fox said.

The elephant disappeared into the mud.

From that day on, the elephant and man became enemies. Man never trusts the pachyderm and that is why he always keeps a spear handy and chains the legs of even the most timid of elephants.

Glossary

Page 15: *Gama Rala:* A village elder who owned paddy lands and commanded respect among the rural folk who elevated him as a leader in an unofficial capacity. As almost every village had a Gama Rala, the stories are not related to one person in particular.

Page 22: *Wangediya:* Mortar. A useful village utensil made of wood or granite to pound rice and other pulses with a pestle. After the grinding mills were introduced the mortar has gone out of use in cities but it is still popular in villages. The base of the mortar is roughly the size of the imprint of an elephant's foot. Hence, the Gamarala's early suspicion that the circular marks left by the elephant in the mud was the work of a wandering mortar!

Page 22: *Molgaha.* Pestle. The rough literal translation of the Sinhala word is milling tree.

Page 23: *Aha:* A common expression that can denote surprise, defiance and mockery.

Page 26: *Kuruniya:* A vessel made of wood or bamboo to measure rice.

Page 33: *Kekiri:* A type of gourd belonging to *Cucumis melo* family. This is a sweet melon, usually consumed fresh for the sweet and juicy pulp. In Sri Lanka kekiri is eaten raw or cooked as a curry to be consumed along with rice.

Page 35: *Kitul: Caryota urens.* The sap of this palm yields toddy (palm wine), an alcoholic beverage, popular in rural areas also for its therapeutic value. The sap of the flower is boiled to make a liquid sugar (*jaggery*) and its trunk pith yields sago that is made into a tasty sweet. Elephants relish its leaves. The tree is as tall as a coconut palm with dark green fronds covering a wide area and dominating the landscape. Its flower is a cascading mass of tresses.

Page 37: *Elowa Gihin Melowa Awa:* This is a widely used idiom in Sri Lanka to describe recovery from a serious illness that could have cost one's life. Sri Lankans often use such colourful idioms in their everyday conversation.

Page 39: *Buffalo curd and coconut treacle:* A traditional and very popular dessert in Sri Lanka. The smoky taste of coconut treacle goes well with extra creamy buffalo yoghurt.

Page 39: *Jack Fruit tree: (Also spelt as Jak Fruit) Artocarpus heterophyllus.* A popular tree in the tropics - known as '*kos*' in Sinhala, '*Palapalam*' in Tamil and '*Chakka Pazham*' in Malayalam. The shreds of the unripe fruit are usually cooked like a curry. The canned tender jack fruit and the sweet bulbs of the ripe ones are available in the West. The seeds can be cooked or boiled and its powder used to make sweet balls called '*kos eta aggala*'. The ripe fruit yields tasty, sweet flesh and is eaten as a dessert. There are two varieties of the ripe fruit. One tree yields hard flesh which is called '*waraka*' in Sinhala while the soft bulbs are produced by a different tree. The fruit of this tree is called '*wela*'. The ripe fruit has a sweet aroma and can be smelled from yards away. The timber of the tree is used to build homes, make household furniture and boats.

Page 46: *Ran Kekiri:* A variety of gourd known as golden melon due to its colour, rarity and sweetness.

Page 43: *Toenail:* In many Sri Lankan folk tales, toenails are featured as something that can kill people when pricked. In another story in the collection there is a she-devil who fixes her toenail and a thumbnail on a door with the intention of killing a girl.

Page 46: *Ayurveda:* An Indian healing system which goes back to 4000 years B.C. It is a popular alternative system of medicare in Sri Lanka today with several Ayurveda hospitals and laboratories in many areas of the country.

Page 51: *Jaffna cigar:* A hand-rolled pungent cigar rolled in the northern Jaffna peninsula of Sri Lanka, from locally-grown tobacco. This is popular among the village folks.

Page 60: *Kevum. Oil cakes:* A deep-fried sweet made from rice flour and palm treacle for ceremonial occasions, particularly during Sinhala New Year.

Page 60: *Aggala:* Balls rolled in hand usually made from ground rice mixed with palm treacle to be consumed with tea. A popular item is one made with sesame seeds, jaggery and scraped coconut.

Page 60: *Kokis:* Another popular Sri Lankan sweet made for ceremonial occasions. A decorative mould is used to dip in a batter before frying it in oil. The origin of this sweet goes back to the Dutch who ruled Sri Lanka during the mid-17th century to the late 18th century. These sweets are made during the Sinhala New Year.

Page 60: *Helapa:* Popular half-moon shaped sweet steam-wrapped in a leaf known as Kenda that adds pleasant aroma.

Page 68: *Jambu: Syzygium samarangense.* Known in English as Java apple, Semarang rose-apple. Also known as Rose Apple, Red Wax Jambu, Plum Rose and Malabar Plum. A sweet fruit with high water content. A native of South and East Asia.

Page 82: *Ambalama:* A traditional one-room resting place constructed by the villagers for weary travellers wanting to rest for the night and continue the journey at sunrise the next day. Before motor vehicles became popular people used to walk or travel in bullock carts. Sometimes a journey would take several days and every village had an *ambalama* to rest for the night. Beggars and mendicants who were wondering seeking charity too occupied them for the nights. *Ambalamas* started disappearing after the 1970s.

Page 83: *Kirala:* Red-wattled lapwings. The bird is native to West Asia and the Indian subcontinent. It is known for its colourful appearance and the loud call, often uttered at night. In some parts of India and Sri Lanka, a local belief is that the bird sleeps on its back with the legs upwards for fear of sky falling down. Some Sri Lankans believe that its cry is a bad omen.

Page 87: *Goraka: Garcinia gummi-gutta.* A dried, very sour fruit that is used as a spice in Sri Lankan and Indian curries. Also known as Malabar tamarind. The redness and round shape of the ripe fruit are often compared to bulging eyes in many Sri Lankan folktales.

Page 88: *Drumstick tree: Moringa oleifera.* In Sinhala the fruit of this tree is known as Murunga and in Tamil Murungai. It is mainly found in home gardens. The fruit is used to make a tasty curry. The leaves are said to lower blood pressure and can be stir-fried. One interesting thing I noticed as a child was people crushing young leaves of this tree, mix it with lime (calcium oxide) and applying it to treat dog bites. The fruit, considered a vegetable, is long like a drummer's stick. Hence the term drumstick tree.

Page 95: *Panchatantra:* Ancient Indian collection of animal fables believed to be written around the 3rd century BCE.

Page 99: *Ayubowan:* Traditional Sinhala greeting that means *May You be Blessed with a Long Life.*

Page 101: *Chi, chi:* A Sinhala expression to show disgust.

Page 109: *Ané:* Oft-heard Sri Lankan expression denoting sympathy or helplessness.

Page 116: *Kenda leaves: Macaranga peltata.* A tree growing in the woodlands. A popular half moon shaped sweet called *Helapa* is flattened on its leaves and steamed, with the leaves enhancing flavours.

Page 117 *Polkichcha:* Oriental Magpie Robin. A common bird in Sri Lanka. Its cry is described as a harbinger of bad luck.

Page 117: *Eraminia:* A shrub with sharp, long thorns common in the woodlands.

Page 117: *Heeraluwa lizard: Ophisops leschenaultii.* A small common skink. Also known as *hikanella* or *sikanella* in Sinhala.

Page 120: *Veddha:* The indigenous people of Sri Lanka who live in the jungles by hunting animals and cultivating seasonal crops. Their numbers are dwindling as their traditional lands are being acquired for agriculture and irrigation. According to historians, they are descended from the children of King Vijaya, an Indian prince who established a prosperous kingdom. The children and their mother, Kuveni, a woman from a native tribe whom the king married, were exiled into the jungle, after King Vijaya decided to marry an Indian princess from the ruling Khastriya-class.

Page 123: *Mee flowers: Madhuca longifolia.* The flowers of a large tree of medicinal value. The flowers have a taste akin to raisins and are used to flavour Helapa sweets. The flowers are fermented to produce a country-liquor called *mahuwa* in certain parts of India.

Page 124: *Sakhra Deva:* The mythological Lord of the Gods. It is said that his seat warms when an injustice is done to some being on the earth, calling for his immediate intervention to save the innocent party and punish the culprit.

Page 137: *Hundu:* The smallest container to measure rice that can hold one to two cups.

Page 140: *Pinthaliya:* A specially made earthen pot full of water kept by the side of the road for travellers to quench their thirst. *Pinthaliya* literally means a charity pot. Today 'pinthaliya', like 'ambalama', have almost disappeared from Sri Lanka mainly due to modern means of transport.

www.ingramcontent.com/pod-product-compliance
Lightning Source LLC
Chambersburg PA
CBHW050755250626
47155CB00005B/2072